Was she going crazy?

She seemed to be in a great, gray-vaulted hall. In the middle of the hall a fire burned, smoldering.

A dark figure squatted over the flames, hands protruding white and bony beneath the flowing black-hooded robe. Between the hands Barbara saw the limp form of some small animal. . . . The soft toneless chant rose to a hypnotic rhythym, a knife flashed, there was a strange small cry. . . .

Whimpering, Barbara drew herself upright. The room, her familiar bedroom, was empty. There was no hall, no shrouded figure, no dead animal. . . .

Then she recoiled in horror. Warm and limp at her side, something . . . *something* . . .

It was there, still warm, the throat still trickling red blood: a large gray mouse, quite dead and not yet cold.

A scream contracted Barbara's throat but never escaped.

What had she done?

Dark
Satanic

Marion Zimmer Bradley

SEVERN
SH
HOUSE

This title first published in Great Britain 1991 by
SEVERN HOUSE PUBLISHERS LTD of
35 Manor Road, Wallington, Surrey SM6 0BW

British Library Cataloguing in Publication Data
Bradley, Marion Zimmer *1930-*
  Dark satanic.
  I. Title
  813.54 [F]

  ISBN 0-7278-4182-3

Printed and bound in Great Britain
by Billing and Sons Ltd, Worcester

Chapter One

THE SIGN ON THE DOOR, IN MODEST GOLD LET-
ters, read JAMES C. MELFORD, MANAGING
EDITOR. The faintly pretty girl at the reception desk smiled, depressed a button, and
murmured, "Mr. Melford? Can you see Mr. Cannon for a few minutes?" She listened a moment,
then smiled again, a little more cordially this
time, and said, "Take a seat, Mr. Cannon. Mr.
Melford will be with you in just a minute."

The man standing before the desk—tall, thin,
and slightly stooped, his face drawn and haggard as if with some overriding worry—turned
away, fidgeting slightly, and lowered his lanky
body onto a plastic sofa. He picked up a magazine but barely leafed through the pages, riffling
them as if he were shuffling a deck of cards, and
put it down again. He stretched his neck to look
around the office, frowning as if he had lost
something there and couldn't quite remember
what.

1

Whatever it was, it wasn't there, or at least his eyes didn't linger on it. There was a small green plastic Christmas tree, decorated with blue glass balls and red-ribbon bows, on the reception desk. In a rack beside the desk were a few dozen brightly colored paperback books, the recent releases of Blackcock Books. His eyes lingered momentarily on two titles near the top of the rack, *The True Story of Witchcraft* and *Voodoo in the Modern World*, by John Cannon. He squeezed his eyes tightly shut, as if in pain, and the girl behind the Christmas tree raised her head momentarily. "Are you all right, Mr. Cannon?"

"Yes—yes, thank you," he said, and reached out a determined arm to pick up the magazine. He held it without opening it, his hands clenched on the edges, as if forcing himself to sit still. The girl's eyes lingered on him a moment, but a ringing phone forced her attention back to the switchboard, and Cannon loosed his grip on the magazine, sighing faintly.

The office door swung open, and a youngish man, his tie loosened at the neck, his thick light hair standing up in crisp curls, stood in the door. His face broke into a hearty smile.

"Hello, Jock, nice to see you. Want to come inside?" He held out his hand. His voice was warm and welcoming, and the clasp of his fingers firm. Cannon, unfolding himself awkwardly from the chair, relaxed a little in a smile and let himself be shepherded inside.

The office was light, bright, and unpretentious, with a big, workman-like desk overflowing with papers and boxes of manuscripts; more manuscripts, in boxes and thick manila envelopes, were piled up in racks and on shelves at both sides. There were brightly garish paintings on the walls, obviously the originals of the book covers of the publishing house, and a small bronze statuette which read, across the base, SCIENCE FICTION AWARD—1967 in a place of honor atop a filing cabinet. One of the colored paintings displayed a green devil with glaring red eyes and enormous horns; Melford saw his guest's eyes linger on it and smiled again, warmly, as he moved around behind his desk.

"Yes, that's *The Devil in America*. It's still one of our best sellers; we're thinking of reprinting it this spring—providing your agent and I can come to some kind of reasonable terms. Sit down, sit down." He took the desk chair and waved Cannon into a chair beside him. "Cigarette? How've you been, Jock? You're looking a bit rocky. When I called your agent last week, he said you'd been in the country trying to rest. What's the matter, fella? People our age shouldn't need to rest!"

In the flow of this cheerful chatter Cannon relaxed, with a nervous smile. "Nothing, I guess. A touch of the Hong Kong flu, maybe. Yes, I went up to Massachusetts for a few days ... I thought maybe I could work better in the quiet. Only after a few days"—he smiled, the shy and self-deprecating smile again—"the quiet started to get on my nerves."

"You sound like my mother," Melford remarked, grinning, "always talking about the good old days. And yet when the power went off last year, and she and Barbara had to cook a few meals with canned heat, or over the fireplace, you should have heard her bitching! I must say

Barbara was a good sport, though. She was asking about you just the other day—Barbara, that is. So what's doing?"

"Problems," Cannon said, a little diffidently.

Melford still looked friendly, but a very faint frown edged his forehead. "If it's money, Jock, this is the slow season, but maybe auditing would okay another advance."

"Oh, good God, no, I'm not broke," Cannon said quickly, "no more broke than usual, anyway. No, I didn't come here about money, Jamie. Like everybody else, I could use it about now, but if that had been what I wanted, I'd have sicked my agent on you." He laughed nervously. "No, no, it's something else. You did get the manuscript of the new book, didn't you?"

"Sure. It's here somewhere." Jamie Melford pulled a large box with the label of one of the larger authors' agencies toward him. He took off the cover and lifted out a bulky typed manuscript. "We ought to do something about that title, Jock; *Witchcraft in New York Today* . . . it's not a bad title, but it's a little cumbersome, and besides, it will remind everybody of William Seabrook—you know, *Witchcraft, Its Power in the World Today*? They'll think they've read it already, and they won't buy it. It's a damn good book, Jock. I enjoyed it . . . forgot to proofread while I was going through it!"

"You read it? Already?"

"Damn right. We'll be buying it—no point in not telling you—we'll probably have a contract for you at the agency before the end of the week. Should have the money in time for you to do your Christmas shopping."

"The fact is," Cannon said, with an air of

taking the plunge, "I'm not quite happy about the book."

Melford pursed his lips. The gesture made him look ten years older and was incongruous in his boyish face. "I don't get it, Jock. It's a fine book—good as anything you've done. Oh, it goes a bit *far*, of course—I can't say I buy all this weird stuff about witch what-do-you-call-'ems, covens, operating right here in New York City—but after all, that sort of sensationalism is what sells books, and I don't think very many people take it seriously, any more than they take Bela Lugosi in *Dracula*, on 'The Late Late Show,' seriously. Except for a few assorted nuts, of course."

"That's the trouble, Jamie," Cannon said. "I seem to have—without realizing it—stepped on somebody's toes. I've been having trouble . . ."

Jamie chuckled. "Oh, I suppose all the local witches are sticking pins in your image," he said.

"I wouldn't be surprised," Cannon said quietly.

Jamie stopped and looked at him. Then he said, "You're serious, Jock?"

Cannon twisted his long nervous fingers. "Yes. I was so damn afraid you'd laugh at me."

"Hell no, man. There are so many assorted nuts in this city, *somebody* is sure to take offense at damn near anything we publish. Do you remember the piece we did about vice on the streets? Believe it or not, some crackpot society calling itself the Sexual Freedom League called me up every day for a week saying that we had set back some sex laws in this country ten years, or some such rubbish. And that biography of . . . oh, what the hell was his name—*you* know, the general that got fired—the John Birch Society

kept calling us up and calling us a pack of dirty
red radicals, and worse things." Jamie smiled
his warm, reassuring smile. "So you're beginning to get the crackpots, too? Hell, it's a compli-
ment . . . shows you're well known. Who bothers
to slander the village idiot?"

Cannon still looked shaken and nervous. He
said, "It seems so *real* somehow. And then, last
week, when I got sick"—his laugh sounded
hollow—"I began . . . wondering."

"Look," Jamie began, but the ringing phone
cut him off. He leaned forward, picked it up,
and said, "James Melford speaking."

Gradually his face darkened and knotted into
a frown. "Yes, Cannon is here now . . . what is
that? *What?* Say, who is this, anyway? Hey,
you—" He stood holding the phone in his hand,
the dial tone faint and buzzing, clearly audible.

"Some damned nut," he said angrily, "some
obscene lout. Is *that* what you've been getting,
Jock?"

"That and more," Cannon said, and then the
floodgates broke. "It started with the phone calls.
Just a nasty whispering voice, neither man nor
woman, just a—a *voice*, threatening me with all
sorts of ghastly things if I finished the book. It's
why I went to the country. I thought I'd get
away from it there. Only then it was letters, and
once a dead chicken on my doorstep—all blood—
and once a picture . . . a picture of a filthy little
doll with pins sticking in it—" His voice broke
and he shuddered.

Jamie looked at him, aghast. "Insane!" he
muttered.

"I've thought I was going insane."

"Good God! I don't mean *you*, Jock. I mean

the filthy bastards who'd do a thing like that. Look, Jock, it's either a complicated practical joke—and about the unfunniest I ever heard of, believe me—or else some lunatic who takes all this stuff seriously has decided to try and gét your goat, break your nerve. But use your head, man! He can't do you any harm with all this hocus-pocus unless you let him get on your nerves!"

"I'm not so sure," Cannon said, still in that quiet voice. "Seabrook took it seriously. He knew of people who had actually been killed by what you call that hocus-pocus."

"Savages . . . superstitious natives who believed in it—I've read his book, too. It can't hurt you unless you believe in it."

"I'm not so sure of that either," Cannon said. "I've been researching and reporting on this kind of thing for five years and eight books now. I am beginning to take it seriously—damn seriously. I think it shows in my books, and I think that's why they're after me."

Jamie Melford looked at his friend with a troubled frown. He was entirely too good-natured to laugh off anything that was troubling the older man this badly; and yet his own inherent skepticism told him it was rubbish. He said, and his voice reflected his dilemma, "Well, Jock, I just don't know what to say to you. I never thought that you, of all people, would let this sort of thing get you down. Wasn't it you who exposed four dozen fake mediums for your first book?"

"Yes," Jock said slowly, "and only later did I begin to realize that there were a few I *couldn't* expose. They couldn't *all* have been simply too clever for me. It only occurred to me later, too, that nobody would bother to fake psychic phenomena without some real psychic phenomena to imitate."

"Well, I can't argue *that*," Melford said, a little impatiently. "It isn't my field. I just know that the books sell well and that there are a tremendous number of people in this country who read everything they can get on the subject—including every new John Cannon. But it's you that's being persecuted—not me. I can laugh off phone calls like the one I just got, but you surely aren't going to let them scare you off, are you, Jock?"

"I hope not. But"—his voice shook a little—"I just don't know what to do. The letter I got this morning . . ."

He rummaged in a pocket and spread a single sheet of paper on the desk. Both men bent over it.

It read, in straggling block printing:

WITHDRAW YOUR NEW BOOK
AND SAVE YOUR LIFE—OR
JONATHAN LAWRENCE CANNON
PREPARE TO DIE.

Melford shook his head, his lips pressed tight in anger. "They seem to know the name you sign your contracts with, for what that's worth" was his only comment.

Cannon's voice was diffident. "I don't suppose you'd want to . . . withdraw the book?"

"Are you out of your head? I said I thought it was your best so far. What does your wife say. about all this, Jock?"

"I've tried to keep it from her," Cannon replied. "All except the dead chicken. She found it and it shook her up. Bess is a good sport, and she traipsed all over Haiti with me for the book on voodoo, so she knew what it meant. Of course, she has only one answer"—he smiled, faintly—"return to the fold. I told her that was just fighting superstition with superstition, as if holy water and a rosary could drive away a curse."

Jamie laughed aloud. "Well, if one's real, the other would have to be real, man," he said. "Maybe you ought to fight fire with fire. They'd have a heck of a time trying to curse you if you were at high mass, wouldn't they?"

Cannon said with a quiet dignity, "I'm not a religious man myself, but I respect Bess's religion too much to pretend in that sort of thing."

Jamie sobered slightly. "I suppose you're right. But I respect reason too much to withdraw the book and let a bunch of nuts scare me off. And I think you do, too, Jock. Why not take a rest? You look tired, and you've been sick, and your nerves are probably shot. Look, suppose I call up auditing tonight and have them shoot you the first advance right away, so you can afford to get away for a few days and get your nerves back in shape. Have a physical checkup; when the doctor says there's nothing wrong, you'll be ashamed of imagining things. It'll be all right, Jock; you'd never forgive me if I let a bunch of nuts scare you off!" He rose, extending his hand. "I've got to chase you off now, fella; I'm meeting Barbara for a cocktail at five. Give my love to Bess and have her call Barbara one of these days—we might get together for dinner. And I'll have them get that check out to you. All right?"

Cannon stood up, hovering indecisively, but

Jamie's reassuring handshake and friendly words evidently made it impossibly hard for him to continue. When the door closed behind him, Jamie Melford shook his head, murmured a soft "Whew! Poor guy! Now I've heard *everything*," and drew the book manuscript toward him again. Smiling, he scribbled a memo to his secretary to arrange the early advance; it gave him genuine pleasure to do a favor for one of his authors, and Cannon's edgy state had moved him deeply.

Outside his office, in the hall waiting for the elevator, Jonathan Cannon pressed his hand to his heart, and his face twisted in pain. He drew the crumpled letter from his pocket and stared at it, then closed his eyes.

Chapter Two

SOME DAYS, BARBARA MELFORD DECIDED, IT didn't pay to get out of bed.

This had been one of those days if there ever was one. There had been the almost-routine clash with her mother-in-law before leaving the house: the older Mrs. Melford just couldn't manage, not *ever*, to restrain some pointed comments about her day, when women stayed home and *managed* their homes. Barbara had somehow managed not to make the comment on the tip of her tongue: with Mrs. Melford around to manage, nobody else could have gotten a fingertip into the managing line. Yet it rankled. Then she'd spent the morning trying to cope with a spoiled and squalling child model who was getting a cold, and the child model's impossible mother. When she finally had the arrangement posed as she wanted it, one of the studio lights burned out and she had burned her fingers changing the bulb. In the afternoon, a sudden rain

11

shower meant that a fashion model had arrived with damp hair that had to be dried and reset before they could go ahead. And to top everything else, she thought she was getting the curse. *Damn it*, she thought, as she shrugged savagely into her pea jacket, *if Jamie and I weren't married, I'd have been pregnant forty times over by now. I don't care—I'm not especially anxious to have a baby with Mother Melford hanging over my belly. But poor Jamie's going to be so damn disappointed all over again, and he'll probably start up again about going back to Dr. Clinton, and she told me, last time, that I should relax and wait another year before going through the whole routine of tests again.*

The icy wind and an off-key rendition of "Joy to the World" by three half-frozen-looking Salvation Army workers, disspiritedly singing in front of the department store at the end of the block, bit at her simultaneously as she emerged into the street. She fished in her pocket for a handful of pennies and threw them into the kettle, realizing just too late that she had thrown her last subway token in with them. Oh, hell and damnation, you just *couldn't* fish it out in front of the poor guys. She walked on, frowning, toward the corner where she usually met Jamie after work.

He was there as usual before her, looking handsome in this thick tweed overcoat and the Astrakhan cap she had given him last birthday, and her heart warmed at the sight. One nice thing about Jamie, he never made any wisecracks about women being late; he knew what it was like in a business where you worked with temperamental people all day long and any one of them could throw you off schedule.

"Hello, darling." She fell into step beside him. "Nice day?"

"Good enough. Let's go out of this wind, shall we? I could use a drink. And you?"

"Coffee, thanks. I think I'm getting my period."

"Oh, hell. I'm sorry, sweetheart." To her great relief, he did not mention Dr. Clinton. They went down the steps into the restaurant, sat down, and gave their orders. Catching sight of their two forms in a mirror over the tables, she thought again how handsome Jamie was and how lucky she was to have him. God knows, plenty of prettier women had wanted him. She saw herself in the plain Navy pea jacket with short tartan skirt and high, fashionable boots, her short crisp dark hair wrapped in a tartan scarf. Barbara, who worked in the fashion world and knew glamour from the inside out, distrusted it as phony and thought of herself as nice-looking rather than beautiful.

The drink for Jamie and the coffee for Barbara arrived, and Barbara loosened her scarf and ran her fingers through her hair. "Oooh, what a day!"

"Rough?"

"Rough. I'm seriously thinking of refusing to work with children under ten. Oh, I know that's not fair—most of them are nice kids, but the occasionally brattish one ... I'm thinking of dropping a word to the agency that I won't have Peggy Andrews again, or at least not with her mother around. The trouble is that she looks exactly, but *exactly*, like the Tenniel Alice, and that seems to be a type that makes editors and art directors go all soft and melty. It's as bad as blond little boys who look exactly like Christopher Robin."

Jamie chuckled. "You've got a whole theory of Jungian archetypes there in few words, darling. But don't tell me that wrestling with one brat got you looking so hag-ridden."

"Oh, no. It was just one damned thing after another all day, that's all, and finding out that I had the curse was just the last straw." She laughed suddenly. "Maybe someone's sticking pins in my image."

"Ouch!" Jamie winced. "Don't *you* start that, Barby."

"What's the matter, dear?" she asked, recognizing distress behind the flippant manner. He said, "Jock Cannon stopped in the office today," and gave her a brief report of Cannon's troubles.

"But that's awful," she said, troubled, "he's *such* a nice man, and Bess Cannon is so sweet. Jamie, you don't think he's in real trouble, do you?"

"Well, I don't think he's bewitched, Barbara. Use your head," Jamie said a little curtly.

Barbara said slowly, "I didn't mean that. But I read an article in the paper today about some girl who was—I mean, who said she was—a witch ... really practicing witchcraft and all that. And then there's that Sybil Leek, who writes books about witchcraft. And all the things in Jock's books ..."

"Ridiculous," Jamie said, laughing. "No, I'm just afraid poor old Jock is on his way to a nervous breakdown. He's a sensitive, impressionable guy, and all those things he writes about are beginning to get him down."

"Oh, no! You mean he's *imagining* all these things? I've *heard* of people writing anonymous letters to themselves and all that—"

"No, no. I don't mean that. I mean that he's taking a goofball persecution, or a hoax, by a batch of screwballs and blowing it up out of all proportion. I don't think they could actually kill anybody with all that rot, but if poor old Jock takes it too seriously, he could wind up in Bellevue cutting out paper dolls."

"Don't!" Barbara winced.

Jamie said quickly, "Sorry! I forgot . . ."

"It's all right. Only poor Jerry . . ." She bit her lip, trying not to remember her only brother. He had had a serious breakdown, and the doctors had suggested hospitalization. Jamie had been willing to pay for a period in a mental hospital, but Mrs. Melford had talked so tellingly about the terrible disgrace to the family if anyone knew that *her* son's wife had an insane relative—of course no one in *their* family had ever been in an insane asylum, as she persisted in calling it—that Jamie had temporized, tried to talk Jerry into "snapping out of it."

Jerry had shot himself four weeks later. Barbara said now, tensely, "Look. I *understand* your mother's point of view. She belongs to a previous generation and doesn't realize times have changed. She was really trying to help me escape what she honestly believed was an awful disgrace. She told me over and over that she was only thinking of poor Jerry's future if anyone ever found out. I've forgiven her, honestly —I'm sure I have. But I only had one brother. And I hope to God that if Jock Cannon is cracking up, Bess Cannon can help him get into a hospital while there's time!"

"Oh, I honestly don't think it will go that far," Jamie protested. "After all, it isn't as if he'd been *imagining* these things. I got one of the calls, too: foulest filthy language you can imagine, threatening me with all kinds of things if I printed Jock's book. But I'm used to that sort of thing and Jock isn't. He needs to get away . . . get some perspective."

But Barbara had gone white. She said, "Suppose they start doing—whatever it is they're doing to Jock—to you, too?"

He laughed softly. "Suppose they do? Let 'em do their worst, honey; it can't hurt me any more for them to curse me than it would for them to pray for me. Come on—this is the modern age! And *I'm* the one who has to read science fiction and horror stories every day!"

She drew breath and asked, "But why would they persecute him?"

Jamie shrugged. "I'm not a psychiatrist, but I suppose there are some nuts in this city who practice witchcraft, or think they do, and don't like Jock making it public. Look, sweetheart, this is a hell of a depressing subject over the dinner table. Let's order a good steak, and to hell with the budget."

She smiled faintly. "That sounds like a wonderful idea."

"Just let me go and call Mother," Jamie said, sliding out of his seat. Barbara said, almost guiltily, "Do you suppose we really ought to ask her to come down and join us?"

He smiled easily. "I don't think so, Barby. I imagine she enjoys having the kitchen to herself

once in a while, just as much as we enjoy being
by ourselves. Just let me call. Back in a minute."

Barbara relaxed, sneaking a sip of Jamie's
drink, thinking about her mother-in-law. She
thought, whimsically, *It's a good thing there aren't
any witches, or Mother Melford would have had
me hoodooed long before this.*

It was so *humiliating*, not to get along with
your mother-in-law. It made you feel like something out of a third-rate TV play, a stock situation, not an intelligent woman at the final third
of the twentieth century.

Jamie slipped back into the seat opposite.
"Mother's fine," he said, "happy as a lark. She
has a guest for dinner herself. It seems Dana
Becker's back in town."

Barbara laughed weakly. "I told you it wasn't
my day," she said, then elaborated on the amus-
ing thought that had come to her while he was
at the phone. "It's a good thing there are no
witches, or Dana would have used some sort of
witchcraft to land you. Lord knows, she did
everything else."

He laughed a little, too. "Oh, come on, Barbara," he protested, "it's not like you to be catty,
and that's all past history. It isn't the poor girl's
fault that Mother was bound and determined I
was going to marry *her* instead of you. After all,
I *did* marry you. And since she's a friend of
Mother's, I expect we'll have to see her from
time to time. And Dana likes you. She told me
so."

I'll bet, Barbara thought, but she had sense
enough to keep the remark to herself. She con-
tented herself with saying, "Well, I don't begrudge Mother her friends, as long as she can't

try to marry you off to them anymore," and left
it at that.

After all, she thought, sticking a fork in her
salad, she had brought Dana to see them herself
the first time. Dana had been sent to her by the
model agency to model a new line of miniskirts,
and had fainted on the floor. Barbara, who knew
how the high-fashion models ruined their health
with crash-dieting and Dexadrine, had sent for
a cup of soup. In the conversation that followed,
finding Dana intelligently interested in the technical side of photography, Barbara had invited
her along on a date with Jamie, who was the
most casual of dates then and not yet a prospec-
tive husband.

It had been a mistake, Barbara thought cyni-
cally, as most feminine kindnesses were mis-
takes. Jamie had discovered that Dana's mother
was an old schoolfriend of his mother's. Dana
paid a courtesy call, and, before Barbara knew
it, Dana was a dear old friend of the family, a
cherished protégee of Mrs. Melford. Barbara had
soon realized, to her horror, that Mrs. Melford
was firmly resolved on Dana for a daughter-in-law.

Jamie was no apron-string son, and he had
held out steadfastly against his mother's storms,
pleas, blandishments, and feminine wiles. Only
Barbara realized what a long hard fight it was,
and, when she and Jamie were safely married
and Mother Melford had given in graciously and
pretended to welcome Barbara, Barbara was not
fooled at all. The older woman disliked her and
had never forgiven her.

Dana had had the decency to leave the city,
but now she was back. Barbara thought, angrily, *If Mother Melford helps that . . . that* witch

to break up my marriage, I'll ... I'll ... She
laughed abruptly and took a bite of her steak.

"What's funny, Barby?"

"I'll have to read Jock's book over again, if
Dana's getting back, and get a love charm so
she can't steal you from me!"

"Attagirl," Jamie said, laughing, and started
to cut his steak.

They lingered over spumoni and black coffee,
and it was nearing nine when a waiter approached the table, a little apologetically. "Mr.
Melford? There is a telephone call for you—I
believe quite urgent. You can take it here at the
table if you would rather."

Jamie looked puzzled as the plug-in phone
was brought and he picked up the receiver. "I
hope Mother isn't sick; no one else would know
I'm here," he commented, and spoke into the
receiver.

The answering voice was wholly unfamiliar.
"Mr. Melford? This is Emergency, at City General Hospital. We have a patient here who was
brought in a short time ago, off the street. We
have identified him as a Mr. Cannon, but we
have no home address or next-of-kin for him,
and the patient is incoherent and keeps calling
for you. We found your home number in his
wallet, and someone there said you could be
reached here."

Jamie said, slowly, "I can give you his home
address ... or would you rather that I call his
wife? Of course, I'll come down if he wants me."

"That's for you to decide, Mr. Melford, but if
you could telephone Mr. Cannon's wife, I would
appreciate it very much. We're rather busy here."

"Could you tell me what—" Jamie began, but the voice had already rung off. He replaced the receiver slowly. "I'll be damned!"

"Jamie, what's the matter?"

"Speaking of the devil," he said. "Poor Jock Cannon—he's been run over or mugged or something. That was the hospital calling. They didn't know his home address but he was carrying our number."

"Jamie, how awful!"

"I should go to the hospital," Jamie said distractedly. "They said he keeps asking for me. Poor, poor devil. I hope it's not too bad. Poor Bess. I should call her . . ."

"She'll be at her wit's end," Barbara said practically. "Why don't I call her, Jamie, maybe pick her up in a cab and go to the hospital with her? There isn't really much you can do there."

"Oh, well, After all, if he's in bad shape . . . I don't know that they have any other relatives in the city, or even very close friends," Jamie said, and Barbara thought, loving him, how like him it was to put himself out for even an acquaintance. He hated hospitals, and yet here he was, ready to go there on a stormy winter night just because a hurt man had mentioned his name. The least she could do was to relieve him of the problem of Bess. She leaned across the table and gave him a quick kiss on the cheek.

"You go along then, darling; take a cab, it's quicker. And don't worry. People get knocked down every day and they're all right again. I'll call Bess and we'll be along presently."

He put on his coat, shrugging it around his shoulders with that inimitable gesture no woman can imitate, and went off, stopping briefly at the cashier's desk to pay the check. Barbara, reaching for her handbag, stiffened herself for the unwelcome task of telling a woman she did not know very well that her husband was hurt and might be dying for all she knew.

As she went to look up the number, it brushed her mind, like a small and unwelcome intruder, that only today Jock Cannon had complained of persecution and fear. *Oh, rats,* she told herself firmly, *you're beginning to think like a detective-story writer. Things like that don't happen in real life. He skidded on the ice, or a hit-and-run driver knocked him down, or a thug conked him on the head for his wallet—and no nonsense, if you please. Things are bad enough without a lot of hysterical rubbish!*

Chapter Three

THERE WAS AN ICY WIND SWEEPING OFF THE EAST River now, and the squally rain earlier in the day had turned to sleet. The steps of the hospital were slick and treacherous, and Jamie skidded, swore, and wondered how in the devil he got into these things.

He found the Emergency entrance, inquired, and heard that Mr. Cannon had been taken upstairs. A very young intern conducted him to the right elevator, and Jamie asked, "What kind of accident was it?"

"Why, I hadn't heard that it was an accident at all; I thought this was a heart-attack case," the intern said. "This elevator will take you right up to the seventh floor, Mr. Melford." Jamie was left wondering what other mix-ups there had been.

The hospital corridor was dark with nightlights and shadows, and a young nurse, her voice hushed to the hour, said that if he was Mr.

Melford she could take him right to Mr. Cannon at once. She led him down silent echoing corridors and past closed doors into a room with the door ajar.

He saw at once that there was a screen around Jock Cannon's bed. They had Jock in an oxygen tent. He was lying against the pillows, his eyes closed, and Jamie thought he was asleep. He sat down uncomfortably in the one stiff chair beside the bed, wondering if Bess would get there in time, if Jock was very bad, if all this was necessary.

Jock moved uneasily on his pillow. His eyes flew open, but they were wild, unfocused; they did not see Jamie. He stirred inside the clear plastic of the tent and muttered, "No, no. Let me go. Don't follow me. What do you want with me?"

Jamie leaned forward, feeling awkward. He took one of the limp hands that lay outside the oxygen tent on the coverlet and said, "Take it easy, old man. You'll be fine now."

"Melford—where's Melford," Cannon muttered. "Got to tell him! Jamie! Jamie!"

"I'm here, Jock," Jamie said clearly.

The wandering eyes focused briefly. Cannon said, "Thought you'd never get here. They got me! Jamie, they got me. I saw the knife in the heart. I felt it! I had to tell you about the book. You've got to withdraw that book."

"Nonsense, man!" said Jamie heartily. "You already told me, don't you remember? But it's all right; you've forgotten, but it's all right. Just rest now, and get yourself well again. Bess will be here in a little while."

"Bess." He stirred uneasily and seemed to gasp

for breath. His face twitched, seemed congested
and dark. "They baptized it—in my name . . .
felt the knife, and then . . . my heart! My heart!"

Delirious, Jamie thought. *He's still thinking
about that foul letter he got. Damn those people,
anyway.* Jock muttered and moaned incoherently;
a nurse came in, checked his pulse, and said in
an undertone, "You must be very careful not to
excite him, Mr. Melford; he's very dangerously
ill."

Jamie nodded and sat back in the chair. The
nurse started to go away. Suddenly Jock struggled upright, clutching wildly at the supports of
the oxygen tent. It wobbled; the nurse hurried
back and steadied it. He gasped for breath, his
face twitching and darkening almost to purple
as he fought, clutching at his chest. Then he
screamed—a long, agonized sound.

"No! No! The knife . . . the knife . . . the de-
mon . . . let me go! Let me go!"

The nurse said in her crisp, professional voice,
"No one is hurting you, Mr. Cannon. You must
lie still now, or we will have to put you in
restraints." Jock did not hear; his arms thrashed
wildly and the nurse reached over and pressed a
bell, hard. Two other nurses came hurrying in;
they took in the situation at a glance, and within
a few minutes Jock lay trussed and motionless,
struggling vainly against the wide straps binding him to the bed. A doctor came in and looked
at the man sternly, then turned to Jamie. "Don't
you know you mustn't excite him?"

Jamie opened his mouth to protest, but the
nurse said firmly. "He didn't say a word, Doctor; I was here. Mr. Cannon just began shouting."

"I don't like to give him any more sedation;

I'm not sure his heart will stand it." The doctor
frowned, bending over the motionless, gasping
form with his stethoscope. After a long time he
straightened and asked, "Did you manage to
contact his wife, Mr. Melford?"

"My wife is bringing her to the hospital."

"Very well. Call me if there is any change,
Nurse." The doctor went away; the nurse stood
for a moment writing on her chart, then took
another chair near the door. There was no sound
in the room but the soft hiss of the oxygen and
the strangled sound of Jock's breathing. Jamie
wished he could go out for a cigarette, but he
didn't like to leave Jock alone in case the older
man should call for him again or recover consciousness.

Minutes ticked by slowly. Then Jock stirred
again. "Jamie! Jamie!" he muttered restlessly.
"I can't see you. Come here."

Jamie glanced uneasily at the nurse. She said
almost soundlessly, her lips moving, "Go to him.
Try to reassure him."

"I'm here, Jock. Bess will be here in a little
while. Barbara's bringing her."

"The book . . . you mustn't——"

"Never mind that now, old fellow. Just rest."

"Damn it," Jock gasped, "listen to me. I'm
dying and I know it. They got me . . . they'll get
you, too. I tried to fight something bigger than I
was, something nobody can fight alone. Go after
them, Jamie, but don't publish it until they're
all gone."

"Jock, you mustn't talk," Jamie protested. "Just
relax."

"Promise you'll get them! Damn it, don't treat
me like a child. I may not be able to talk much

more! I wrote too much ... chapter five ...
Father Mansell ... Houston Street. They may
have killed Lucille, too." His eyes fluttered shut,
twitched open again. "Promise! Promise me,
Jamie. Don't let them kill anyone else."

Helplessly, with a sick feeling of humoring
a madman, Jamie said, "Of course I promise.
You'll be better when Bess comes."

The nurse said softly from the door, "Mrs.
Cannon is here, Mr. Melford."

Behind him the soft, gentle voice of Bess Cannon
said, "Should I disturb him now, Nurse?"

The nurse looked straight at her. She said, "I
don't think it makes any difference now, Mrs.
Cannon. You'd better go to him."

Jamie turned. "Bess." He held out his hand
and led her to the bed.

"Jock, dear," she said, very softly.

His eyes rested briefly on her. He smiled and
lay still, and Jamie, thankfully, withdrew toward
the door.

He had seen Bess Cannon less than half a
dozen times and had spoken to her less than a
hundred words. She was a short, soft, sandy-
haired little woman, rounded, round-cheeked,
verging on middle age, and somehow gently
blurred in appearance, peaceful and plain. Now
she looked tired and as if she had been crying,
but she was composed, and Jamie was grateful:
he had been almost prepared for hysterics.

She turned her head and said in a gentle undertone, "Don't think you have to go, Jamie.
But perhaps you'd better bring the priest ... I
spoke to the doctor."

But Jock isn't a Catholic, Jamie thought. Then
he remembered that Jock in his delirium had

unlocked the door of their Village apartment. They had delayed to talk to the doctor, to stand by while Bess signed the necessary papers, to take Bess home in a taxi, and to telephone Jock's surviving sister in Connecticut.

Barbara had offered to stay with her, but Bess, quite composed by now, had refused. She said that Jock's sister, Margaret, would be there on the earliest train, and she would be quite all right. So at last they had left her and found a cruising cab to drop them at the door.

Barbara, hanging up her coat in the tiny foyer, thought that the whole evening seemed nightmarish, not quite real. One moment Jamie was talking about Cannon's delusions of persecution, the next, with the speed of the incredible, the summons and his death had come. Not that she believed in witchcraft, but it gave her a creepy feeling. Jamie looked gray and exhausted, and she took his coat gently and hung it up. "Do you want a drink before you go to bed, darling? Hot milk . . . anything?"

"I'll sleep without it." Jamie took her arm and walked into the tiny living room—and stopped, blinking. Barbara, too, stopped in momentary confusion, then irritation. The double bed had been opened out from the sofa, and on it, covered with a light afghan, lay a woman, sleeping, only a mass of fair hair and the neck of a blue flannel nightgown. Then Dana Becker sat up, blinking, fair hair faintly luminescent in the light from the streetlight outside the window.

"Oh . . . Barbara. I'm sorry, I was asleep." She shook her head faintly. Barbara, pressing back a frown by brute force (*This was absolutely all I needed!*) said, with what she hoped was

mentioned a Father Mansell. People in serious illness were likely to revert to former patterns. He said, "Of course, Bess," and went quietly out down the hall to the nursing station. He said, "Mr. Cannon wants to see Father Mansell."

The nurse blinked slightly. "Father Mansell? He wants his own priest? We'll be glad to call him, if you'll give us the number, but perhaps, if he's very ill, I should call our own chaplain? Father Masters would be glad to come, I'm sure, and he could be here in six or seven minutes. The rectory is right down the block at Our Lady of Perfect Peace."

"Yes, yes, of course."

"And then Mrs. Cannon can call her own parish priest later, if she wishes. I'll call the Father right away," the nurse said, picking up a telephone, and Jamie started back toward Jock's room. Barbara stepped out of the waiting room and beckoned to him. "How is he, Jamie?"

"Not very good, Barbara, I'm afraid. They've sent for the priest. He was delirious; they had to put him in restraints," Jamie said, forcing his mind away from Jock's words. Madness, yes, but frighteningly coherent.

Damn it, *could* a bunch of crackpots kill a man, in this day and age, with their witch doctor lunacies. . . . even if he subconsciously feared them and he believed in their power?

No. Vicious suggestion was possible, yes; anyone who would try to do that to a man—hanging was too good for them. But that would be coincidence, perhaps aggravating the strain in Jock Cannon's heart, but not causing it. No.

If I believed that, life would be insane, chaotic. Impossible.

"Tired, Barbara? You can take a cab home if you want to. I'll stay with Bess in case . . ." His voice trailed off. Not till now had he found himself realizing that Jock was going to die.

"You'd better go back and see if she needs anything."

A sudden cry split the hospital corridors, a ghastly, throat-searing scream. Jamie gasped, "Bess!" and hurried toward the door, but as he entered the hospital room he saw that Bess stood quietly, holding the hand of Jock, who had struggled upright.

Jock screamed again, a cry of agony, terror, and fear. "Devils! No, no, not my soul. The knife . . . the knife . . . they've killed me! They're going to kill me! I see them . . . the knife . . . ah!"

He fell back limp on the pillow. The doctor hurried forward and bent over the bed, rudely thrusting Bess away. Then he straightened up, no longer in a hurry.

"I'm sorry, Mrs. Cannon," he said, softly, "but you must have been expecting this. His heart— had he been ill very long?"

Bess stared at him, her face slowly melting and coagulating in a different shape. She said, swallowing, "Doctor, are you crazy? He was never sick a day in his life. He had a complete physical checkup two weeks ago—for some insurance, he said. The doctor told him—I was there, I heard him—that he had the heart of a man thirty years younger. I—I simply can't believe it."

Neither could Jamie, his head spinning. *No wonder Jock hardly listened when I suggested he have a physical checkup*, he thought numbly.

But if two weeks ago his heart was perfectly sound . . .

Bess said, "He was afraid. Doctor, is there any way anyone could have done this?"

"No. No, it was his heart, Mrs. Cannon," the doctor said soothingly.

"But it *couldn't*—they've killed him," Bess said wildly. "He was afraid. He kept saying they'd get him sooner or later . . ."

A soft, masculine voice asked from the door "Can I help?" and Bess turned to see an oldish man in a Roman collar, carrying a small brief case. He set it down and shook his head. Be said numbly, "He's dead, Father. He died—ju a minute ago."

The priest moved to the bedside, made sign of the cross. He murmured softly in La closed the dead man's eyes, and signed his br with the cross. Then he turned back to them. said, "I'm so sorry, Mrs. Cannon. I came as s as they called me."

"He wasn't a Catholic," Bess said numbl always hoped . . . Father, Father, they k him—with Black Magic—they killed Jock! killed him." Her voice began to rise, high shrill, and the priest stepped forward q and took her arm.

"Come, come, you must not say such bl: mous things in the presence of the dea said sternly, and Bess subsided, breathin; She went to Jock's side. He lay peaceful, empty, and she crossed herself, her fac and turned away. Her mouth worked, said nothing, letting the priest lead he the room.

It was after two when Jamie and

adequate cordiality, "Hello, Dana. I hadn't expected to find you here or we'd have been quieter coming in."

She smiled her pretty and deprecating smile. "Oh, for goodness' sake don't think about *that*, Barbara! You had no way of knowing! I *told* Mom Melford I'd only be in the way, but she really wanted me to stay. You know how she hates being alone."

Barbara didn't know any such thing, and she had forgotten quite how much Dana's addressing of the older woman as Mom annoyed her, even though it was at the older Mrs. Melford's wish; but after all, she couldn't eject a nightgowned guest at two in the morning. She said, "Well, go back to sleep, Dana. I'm sorry we disturbed you; we'll be quiet getting to bed."

She didn't lie down again. The modest nightgown, buttoned close around her neck and at least five sizes too big for her (evidently one of Mrs. Melford's), gave her the childlike look of a small girl in her mother's clothes. "You're so late, she was worried! Were you in an accident?"

Jamie said, "No, but a friend of ours was taken ill and I had to go to the hospital to identify him, and it's a miserable night for that."

"Yes, I was worried," said the older Mrs. Melford from the doorway. A small, almost frail figure, with hair in a long lank plait down her back and engulfed in a heavy fleece robe of nondescript pink, her face worked with emotion. "Why didn't you call, Jamie? I was seeing you lying dead in the street; I was thinking of calling all the hospitals."

"No, Mother, it's all right, only I just couldn't get to a phone," Jamie said, and Mrs. Melford pursed her lips. "And *Barbara* couldn't phone either?"

"I was with the man's wife,. Mother," Barbara said, hating herself for feeling on the defensive. She felt like a cruel daughter-in-law conspiring to keep an old lady worried.

Dana said, wide-eyed, "I hope the poor man is all right."

"Well, it depends on how you look at it," Jamie said curtly. "He's dead."

"Anyone I know?" Mrs. Melford asked.

"No. One of my writers," Jamie said. "And if you don't mind, I'd like to get to bed. I'm pretty tired, and I do have to work tomorrow."

"I shouldn't have asked Dana to stay," Mrs. Melford said wearily. "It only slows you down on your way to bed, keeps you awake, gets in your way . . ."

"Oh, Mother," Barbara said impatiently, "nobody minds if you have guests, anytime, you know that. Dana's perfectly welcome to stay as long as she wants to. We'll be hospitable in the morning when we're not so tired, that's all." She went into the bedroom, biting her lip, and closed the door, knowing she had lost her temper again and that Jamie was watching his mother's brave effort to look kindly and courageous in the face of his wife's nasty temper. *She does it every time,* Barbara thought. Then, smiling, a little wryly, she began to brush her hair, thinking, *If I'm not careful, I'll have delusions of persecution like poor Jock.*

She slept badly, her dreams interlaced with Bess Cannon's tragic face and the wild outcries of her accusations, and, waking with a start once, she heard Jamie muttering incoherently

in his sleep and knew that he, too, was struggling against nightmares. She woke late, reluctant to face a cold, wretched, gray day and the
cheerful face of Dana at the breakfast table in a
too-big borrowed housecoat of her mother-in-
law. Mrs. Melford, who made a virtue of early
rising, was presiding over the electric percola-
tor, and Barbara, for the hundredth time, made
the uncharitable comment to herself that this
prevented her from breakfasting in privacy with
Jamie, and remorsefully reminded herself that
after all, the older woman couldn't be expected
to break the habits of a lifetime and sleep late
just for her, Barbara's, convenience.

She accepted a cup of coffee and asked Dana
for the sugar bowl, hoping the matter-of-factness
would do in place of hospitality. Jamie came in,
scowling, weary, and with at small razor-cut on
his right cheek.

Mrs. Melford handed him his coffee and bent
over the back of his chair to kiss his forehead.
"You never did tell me about the poor man last
night, Jamie."

"Nothing to tell. He died of a heart attack,"
Jamie said, "but it may snarl up negotiations
for his next book, since the contract isn't signed
yet. Come to think of it, this is a community-
property state, so Bess can sign the contract
right away. She can probably use the money for
the advance, too. Hell of a note that it should
have to go for Jock's funeral, though."

"Anyone whose books I've read, dear?"

"John Cannon. He does popularizations of
witchcraft and the like."

Mrs. Melford said, with a shudder, "So unwholesome! Such *morbid* stuff! Why do you have to publish such things, Jamie?"

"Because they sell damned well," Jamie said with a sigh. "Stick a piece of toast in the toaster for me, will you, Barbara? I'm going to be hellishly late to the office."

Dana was bent over her coffee cup, as if, Barbara thought unkindly, she was going into a trance over it. Why, she asked herself, should Dana look more vampish in an old robe four sizes too big than she would in a slinky dress and oodles of makeup? I could fight her if she tried looking *sexy* around Jamie. It would be obvious and I could laugh at it. This way, it seems paranoid when I even *think* of it.

The telephone rang and Dana seemed to start all over, to come out of her trance with a shudder. Barbara asked, "Is it for you, Dana? Were you expecting a call?"

"What? Oh, no, I—no, not that I know of," she said, raising a clear untroubled forehead. It rang again, and she said plaintively, "Did you want me to answer it for you, Jamie?"

"I'll go," Barbara made a long arm over the kitchen counter for the extension. "James Melford's residence."

"Mrs. Melford? Is Jim there? Can you put him on? It's Wayne," said the young voice at the other end of the line, and Barbara handed the phone to Jamie. "Sounds like trouble at the office, Jamie."

Jamie took the phone. He listened a moment, then said incredulously, "The *hell* you say," and shook his head. "I'll be right down," he said, and rose precipitately. He said into the phone, on the run, "Did you call the police? Well, why the devil not?" and hung up, striding toward the closet.

"Jamie?" she said, questioningly.

"The office was broken into last night," Jamie said, jerking his coat from the foyer closet and swallowing his coffee in two scalding gulps, "and just one thing seems to be gone."

And before Barbara actually heard the next words, she knew what they would be. She seemed to hear them echoing: "Jock's manuscript."

Chapter Four

THE OFFICES OF BLACKCOCK BOOKS WERE NOT too large to start with, and the addition of two large uniformed policemen crowded Jamie's office to the limit. In the anteroom outside, the book rack had been overturned, and Jamie's secretary was looking at the scattered paperbacks on the floor, obviously itching to pick them up. Evidently the policeman had asked her to leave everything as it was until they had finished their investigation.

Jamie finished going through the material on his desk. Finally he looked up at the policeman. "Nope. Nothing else seems to be missing: just that one manuscript."

"Value?" the policeman asked matter-of-factly.

"That's a hard question, actually. We were intending to pay Cannon three thousand for the paperback rights, which means that if it doesn't turn up or there isn't a carbon copy somewhere in his house, the Cannons have lost that much at least. We hoped, of course, to make a good deal more than that on it; our original print order on a Cannon book is usually something like seventy-five thousand, at seventy-five cents a copy. It's a fairly valuable property, as you can see," Jamie said, but his mind was not on it. He was thinking,

God help us, they meant what they said. They're— whoever they are who were trying to scare Jock to death—they're out to stop that book's being published at any cost.

"Do you know anyone who has a a grudge against you, Mr. Melford?" the younger patrolman—he was dark and slim, the older one burly and tall—asked.

"A grudge? Oh." Jamie looked at the savagely slashed blotter on his desk, the torn picture of Barbara, the broken desk-pen set, and ripped-up calendar. He said, "Oh, I see. The desk set isn't worth ten dollars, but the idea that anyone would do it—no, I can't think of anyone. I mean, I don't suppose everyone loves me, especially authors whose manuscripts I have to reject, but mostly people take that in a very professional manner." He bit his lip, wondering if the policeman would think him crazy if he said what he was thinking.

"Can you get in touch with the author, Mr. Melford?"

Jamie shook his head. "Not unless I employ a medium. He died last night. I was there."

The policeman pricked up his ears. He said, "Last night? Have you any reason to suspect foul play, Mr. Melford?"

"Of course not," Jamie said, irritably. "He died of a heart attack, in City Hospital, with half a dozen doctors and the best of care. But it's a nasty coincidence, and I'm thinking ... the grudge may have been against John Cannon."

"How do you mean that?" the young policeman asked carefully. He wrote something down in his notebook with a ball-point pen.

"He'd been worried," Jamie said slowly, choosing his words, "because some ... some cranks had been molesting him with phone calls and harassing him, trying to get him to withdraw this book. They had played some ... some nasty juvenile pranks on him."

"Sounds like malicious mischief," said the policeman, and wrote again.

"Come to think of it, I got one of the calls too," Jamie said slowly, "yesterday."

"Threats? Did the caller use any threats?"

"He certainly did," Jamie said, tight-lipped.

"This is a weird one," the policeman said slowly. "Just what sort of threats, Mr. Melford? What did he say?"

"I don't use that kind of language," Jamie said with a glance at his secretary, who was all ears, "but in general he threatened me with all sorts of obscene bodily harm and indicated that I'd be in no condition to—to raise a family."

The policeman's mouth twitched, either in disgust or nervous embarrassment, and he said, writing it down, "I'll just put down 'threatened mayhem, to wit, castration.' Will that do?"

"That's close enough," Jamie said.

"Now. Where can I talk to—did the deceased author have a wife, a family?"

"Only his wife. They had no kids," Jamie said, "and she could back up this story of persecution: I gather they were throwing dead animals and similar garbage on his doorstep." He thought, his mouth tight, *Damn it, I've got to get Bess's copy of that thing—she told me once that Jock always made three carbons—and find out just what was in it that's got these lunatics running scared. And then, damn it,* he was plotting to himself, excitedly, *how can I use this for publicity? If this is the kind of book that anyone—even a group of crackpots—would stop at nothing to keep out of print, maybe that would be a good publicity campaign!*

He felt vaguely ashamed of himself for the thought crossing his mind: *Now if they had murdered Jock, that would really be a story. . . .*

Yes, and I'd give it all up to have poor Jock walk into this office right now, damn it.

He signed the complaint form the police proffered, charging a person or persons unknown with grand larceny, breaking and entering in the night, malicious mischief, use of obscene language over the telephone, harassment, and threats of grievous bodily harm. "I'm assuming this is all tied in together," the policeman said, "and I'll want to talk to Mrs. Cannon, although if her husband died within the last few hours she probably won't want to see us right away. We'll be in touch with you, Mr. Melford."

"Can I have this place cleaned up now?"

"Sure, we're done with it," the second policeman said as they left, and Jamie told his secretary, "Clean this mess up," but sat at his desk, arms crossed on the ruined blotter, scowling. He had to get the other copies of that manuscript and lock them in the office safe right away, just in case the unknown persecutors had other ideas. He had to call the newspapers—or at least he should consult the publisher, one Andrew Burns, who, for all practical purposes, was Mr. Blackcock, about using this for publicity. He could harldy have Bess paged at the funeral home . . . wait, he had it. He buzzed his secretary, who scrambled up from the books on the floor, and said, "Leave that there and get me the Merritt Conners Agency on the phone right away. I want to speak to whoever handles the Cannon account."

Talking to Roy Merritt ten minutes later, he lost no time, after brief condolences were exchanged on Jock's death, asking, "You've got a carbon of Cannon's latest?"

Roy Merritt chuckled cagily. "Good thing I'm an ethical man, Melford; it could be that Jock's stuff will have a vogue after his death. A man called me just this morning—it was in the papers, you know, about Jock, just a line on page twelve— suggesting that maybe someone would outbid you for the latest manuscript and that I should hold on to it for a few more weeks."

"Yeah." Jamie felt that he might have anticipated that. "Well, don't hold your breath. I think I know what was behind that. Someone called me and tried to tell me I ought not to handle it."

Merritt listened to the story in silence. Then he said, "Did it ever occur to you that Jock was slipping a little, getting old?"

"Frankly, no," Melford said irritably. "The latest book is as good as any."

"Except that he seems to have begun believing it," Merritt said, "or seemed to. Of course, Jock was a smart cookie. He used to be a publicity agent, you know; I wouldn't have put it past

him to try and stir up interest in the book by
some such stunt as this. Did that ever occur to
you?"

It hadn't, and after a stunned moment, Jamie
dismissed the idea. He said dryly, "He surely
didn't break into this office after he died, did
he? That is, unless something *really* supernatural is going on."

The agent shrugged. "Cannon was a good guy,
God rest him; he might have thought it was a
fairly harmless way of creating some publicity.
But are you suggesting that they may start trying
to get after my copy, too?"

"I don't know," Jamie said slowly. "I wish I
did. But if I were you, Merritt, just in case Bess
loses her copy, I'd suggest that you stick yours
in your office safe. Something damned peculiar
is going on, and I'd rather sound like a damned
old fussbudget than let these characters have
the satisfaction of keeping this book out of print."

"Hey, hey," Merritt said, "you're *serious* about
all this!"

"You're damned right I am!"

"You don't think—good God, you don't think
someone *did* manage to murder Jock?"

"I don't," Jamie said through his teeth, "unless they scared him to death, and considering
that he seems to have started believing it, I
guess they could have. But anyone who would
talk about such a filthy thing and *try* to do it,
especially if they believed they really could, is
somebody I'd love to raise hell with. And if I can
stick a spoke in their wheels, believe me, I'm
going to do it."

"I guess so," Merritt said slowly. "It would be
bad enough to try and throw a scare into some-

body like that even if you didn't believe in it. If you believed it—hanging's too good!"

When Merritt had hung up, Jamie sat back, trying again to remember Cannon's confused last words. Chapter five. He made a mental note to read that chapter with special care. He had spoken of a Father Mansell, too. Jamie pulled down the Manhattan telephone directory and began running through the *M* section.

There were seven Mansells, all the way from Anthony J. to Roberta, M.D. Turning to the Yellow Pages for CLERGYMEN: CATHOLIC, he found none listened. But all clergymen did not have a separate Yellow Pages listing, and he might be a curate at some rectory—or an Episcopalian or Orthodox priest—and not have a separate listing. After a moment's hesitation, Jamie telephoned the number of a priest he had met once in reference to publishing one of their rare religious books.

Although surprised, Father Cassidy expressed his pleasure at hearing from Jamie again. "Can I do something for you?"

"Technical question, really. Is a Father always listed in the Yellow Pages as a priest?"

"Why, no, not unless he asks to be, usually. Why? Are you checking up on something for a novel?"

"As a matter of fact, no: I'm trying to locate a friend of a friend," Jamie said. "Is there a Father Mansell in the diocese?"

"Mansell." The priest repeated the name slowly; then his voice sharpened. "What makes you ask?"

"As I said, friend of a friend. A friend of mine just died and asked me to notify Father Mansell."

Jamie mentally crossed his fingers; that might
have been Jock's intention.

"I see. There *was* a Father Mansell, down at
Saint Barbara's rectory. He isn't there now."

"It's not a common name, but—don't tell me
he's dead too?" Were all the trails going to end
in blind alleys?

"Not exactly," Father Cassidy said. "As a matter of fact, it's rather a ticklish business; Father
Mansell left the Church some time ago. I don't
know where he is now."

Jamie felt a slight gruesome shiver; he remembered from one of Cannon's earlier books
that a major component of the Black Mass was
an unfrocked priest. He told himself not to be
imaginative, but nevertheless he asked, "Then
this man is . . . an unfrocked priest?"

"A picturesque term, and not the one we use
today," Cassidy said, as if he were repressing a
frown. "We prefer to say that he has been
laicized—forbidden to administer the sacraments,
restored to the laity."

"Then he isn't a priest anymore?"

"A priest is always a priest. But you could say
he has been excommunicated. But I must not
gossip: he was a friend of your friend? Catholic?"

"No," Jamie said, "a writer. I gather this
Mansell had helped him in some research, or
something like that."

"And you wanted to notify him of your friend's
death? I don't know if he's still in the city,"
Cassidy said slowly, "but there can be no harm
. . . his first name was Walter, as I remember. I
can't remember the initial; I knew him only
slightly."

But after Jamie had hung up again and was

pondering what to do with this information—
there was no Walter Mansell in the Manhattan
phone book—his phone rang and he heard the
voice he had been half expecting, and dreading,
all that morning. "Jamie? I'm so sorry to bother
you, when you've been so good. This is Bess . . ."

"Don't worry about it. What can I do for you?"

The voice was high, frantic, now blankly terrified. "They've started on me! Oh, God, the phone
rang, and they said . . . they said . . . they said
they'd killed Jock and now it would be . . . it
would be me."

Incredulously, Jamie shook his head. He said,
anger slowly consolidating inside him, "Did you
tell them you haven't the manuscript anymore,
that I have it?"

"I . . . they knew everything . . ." Bess's voice,
at the far end of the wire, faded and broke suddenly into sobs. "It's so nasty, so ridiculous.
They said they'd got your copy and now they
want mine. I'm supposed to put it outside my
door tonight and not look out, not sign the contract . . ."

Jamie felt his rage crystallize into action. He
reached for his checkbook, the phone still tucked
under his chin. He said, "I hate to talk business
with Jock still unburied, but you can't keep this
up, Bess. I'm coming over and bringing a contract with me. You can sign it and give me all
the copies you have."

Bess quavered. "Aren't you afraid . . ."

"I'm no more afraid of those . . . those lunatics . . . than I am of the wind blowing." Jamie
said, hoping he sounded firmer than he felt.
"Hold the fort till I get there, Bess, and have all
Jamie's copies ready for me. If you want them

for souvenirs, I'll see that you get them back once the book's in print. Right now, *I'll* take them over, and they can do their damnedest!"

He hung up again—it seemed suddenly that he had been on the phone all morning—and told his secretary to make out a standard form for a contract for Jock's latest book. With it under his arm, he left the office hearing the phone ring again and not realizing, until he was out of earshot, that he had been half-consciously expecting, every time it rang that day, to hear the sneering, sadistic tones of the call he had gotten yesterday.

He was not looking forward to talking to Bess in her fresh bereavement, or talking business wth her, far less that he might be accused of driving a hard bargain with a newly widowed woman, but this could not be allowed to go on. There were laws against this sort of thing, but they were hard to enforce—a girl he knew had cringed under obscene phone calls for four months and had finally had her phone taken out—and it was better if the manuscript was out of Bess's hands. He thought firmly, *They'll have a hard time scaring* me *off.*

He left the Cannon apartment a couple of hours later as the icy chill of the December dusk was falling. Two thick boxes, which had originally held typing paper and now held two copies of Cannon's manuscript, were under his arm. He felt ragged and exhausted; Bess had been so red-eyed, so haggard, so frayed-looking, and yet so brave and quiet. He wanted a drink, a good dinner, and to forget the whole thing for a considerable length of time. And yet, as he pushed the button to take him up to his apartment, he

knew that he wanted to read through the manuscript again, this time much more carefully.
The first time he had read it as an editor, judging its appeal for his large audience. This time
he was just plain curious; he wanted to know
what was in it to cause even a lunatic to threaten
the writer, and the publisher, and the writer's
wife, so crudely. And Jock Cannon's last words,
almost, before he had dissolved into the delirium before his death, had been "chapter five."

Jamie wanted a long, critical look at chapter
five.

He realized he was too tired to make much
sense. A near-sleepless night, and the stress of
today. *A little more of this,* he thought edgily,
and I'll be believing that Jock died because *they
threatened him—or even that they killed him with
their mumbo-jumbo. Bess already half believes it.*

He remembered that her hand had shook as
she signed the contract, but now he legally owned
the manuscript—or at least Blackcock Books did.

The apartment foyer was warm and welcoming, with a good smell in the air wafting
through from the kitchen and Barbara curled
up on the living-room couch, covered lightly
with an afghan.

She sprang up to kiss him. "No, I'm not sick
or anything; I just felt so tired and droopy this
morning, that I only went into the studio for an
hour or two and canceled this afternoon's appointments. Mother said she'd get dinner and
for me to rest." Standing on tiptoe she whispered in his ear, "Dana's still here."

"Oh, well . . ."

Barbara said swiftly, "I don't mind, really. I
think Mother's lonesome. Maybe she'll get inter-

ested in marrying Dana off to somebody. Are
there any nice bachelors in your office, Jamie?"

"Not over twenty years old," Jamie grinned,
tossing the typing-paper boxes that held the
manuscript (the damned albatross!) on the sideboard. Here, anyhow, they were safe. "There's
Brandon, though—he's divorcing Sue—do you
think Dana would like having fifteen-year-old
twin stepdaughters?"

"Oh, hush," Barbara squealed, holding on to
him, "she'll hear you." And then she sobered.
"Jamie, did you have the feeling this morning
that Dana was *waiting* for the phone to ring?"

"Hell, no. But I was waiting for it myself. I
think I was expecting some more trouble. We
seem to be up against a batch of psychos, Barbara, but for God's sake let's not talk about it
now. I've had the thing on my mind all day,
now it's over there"—he pointed at the two
typing-paper boxes on the sideboard—"and it
can stay there until I've had a drink, a dinner,
and dry feet. What's the matter with you, woman?
Where are the pipe and the slippers?"

Barbara laughed, turning away. "Would Scotch
do instead?"

Dinner was a hearty meal, the thick and fra-
grant lamb stew exquisitely calculated to the
icy weather, and Jamie felt his nerves smoothing
out and easing as he listened to the women,
easily and without friction, chatting about herbs
and spices. Even his mother was more pleasant
than usual to Barbara, saying that she had hoped
to be able to teach her more about the use of
herbs.

"I wish I knew more," Barbara said, "but my
cooking is so simplified. I know, Mother, it

doesn't come up to yours, but let's face it; what can you do with a grilled steak that's better than just putting black pepper on it? Herbs and fancy sauces are for more complicated foods, and I haven't gone that far with it yet."

"Herb lore is very old," Dana said. "I've always been fascinated by it, even though I don't cook much. Mother Melford's taught me everything I know."

"Somebody's sure to benefit some day," Jamie said jovially. "I never knew a man who wasn't a sucker for a woman who can cook. This stew is marvelous, Mom," he added punctiliously.

"And you won't have anyone to fall over in the living room tonight," his mother said. "I've made up the couch in my room for Dana. You don't mind if she stays here while she's apartment-hunting, do you?"

"Oh, Mother Melford." Dana said helplessly. She looked frail and lovely in a jet-black sweater and skirt. "You shouldn't say it like that. What on earth would poor Jamie say if he *did* mind?"

"Of course we don't mind," Barbara said, and only Jamie noticed that her smile was faintly forced. "In fact, Dana, I'll probably be able to get you a commission or two. And Mother will enjoy having company sometimes when I'm out. Maybe she can teach you about herbs then. You're probably a better pupil than I would be. My memory isn't what it ought to be; I'm barely able to remember that you put ginger in gingerbread and garlic in tomato sauce. In fact, all I *really* remember about garlic is from *Dracula*: it keeps away vampires or something, doesn't it, Jamie?"

"I should think it would keep away *anybody*,"

Jamie laughed, "or haven't you ever ridden the subway in the middle of August? No wonder there aren't any vampires in New York, with all the spaghetti joints breathing out garlic into the air. Come to think of it, Jock said something about garlic in one of his books."

"I must be part vampire, then," Dana laughed, "because I detest garlic, and not even the best deodorant can handle the smell. I know it's supposed to be *healthy* or something . . ."

"Don't a lot of Italians believe in the evil eye? Is that why they eat so much garlic in their salami and spaghetti?" Barbara asked. "Maybe they believe it keeps away the evil eye pr——"

"Barbara!" Mrs. Melford shuddered. "We're *eating*! Can't you think of some subject more pleasant for a dinnertime conversation than *vampires*?"

Barbara chuckled. "Sorry, Mother. I sort of like the idea of vampires. All I know about them is Bela Lugosi in the old movies on 'The Late Late Show,' and personally I thought he was kind of cute—cuter than Valentino. He can have my blood anytime. Sorry, Mother, I don't mean to upset you."

Dana broke in tactfully. "I remember the spices and herbs from winter baking at home, when I was a little girl."

"Mmmm," Barbara said, "me too. My mother used to make German *Lebkuchen* and all sorts of spicy Swedish cookies for Christmas. I want my kids to grow up with all that wonderful tradition behind them. Jamie, we're going to have to shop for a Christmas tree pretty soon."

Mrs. Melford's mouth tightened slightly. "I should think in this modern day certainly, Barbara, you aren't going to have a house full of superstitious mumbo-jumbo! No one in this day and age takes religion that seriously."

"Christmas isn't just a religious holiday," Jamie interposed, hoping to avoid the inevitable clash, but Barbara sounded angry. "I'm not a religious person, but I wish I were, and I want my children brought up to respect religion."

Mrs. Melford bit her lip, looking first at Jamie and then at Barbara, but at last she said only, "Time enough to worry about that when you have children," and started to clear away the plates.

Barbara sat staring down at her plate, not speaking. Finally she said, "You brought work home from the office today, Jamie?"

"Yes, I really do have to look through . . ." Jamie found he didn't want to mention it, and amended, ". . . some manuscripts. I'm sorry; I'd like to spend the evening sociably. But what with the tie-up at the office . . ."

"Of course you must," Barbara said swiftly. "Why not make a nice big fire and mix yourself a drink and get started. It's such a miserable cold night out there, a fire's just what you need."

Jamie assented, liking the primitive hominess of the sound. A blazing hearth, a good drink, a quiet room; it would make light of the nonsense he had been thinking earlier, born of nerves and an empty stomach. He kissed his mother lightly on the forehead as she came back for the plates. "Your stew would drive away anyone's collywobbles, Mother. It's great."

"Let me do the dishes, Mother," Barbara said. "You cooked dinner."

"No, I insist," Dana said. "It's more than fair.

You stay here, Barbara, and have a drink with
Jamie before he settles down to work. How is
your headache?"

Barbara shrugged, kneeling to lay the fire.
"About the same. I took some aspirin, but it
doesn't seem——"

"You ought to see a doctor, Barbara dear,"
Mrs. Melford said, standing in the kitchen door
with the soap in her hand. "Not only for that——"

"Its nothing, Mother. Don't fuss. Jamie, will
you get me a match?"

After a vain search on the mantelpiece, Jamie
went into the kitchen for one. As he pushed the
louvered kitchen doors, he heard Dana say ear-
nestly, "Something's simply *got* to be done,
Mother," and Mrs. Melford replying, "Trust me,
dear; I'll manage." She whipped around, then
visibly relaxed: "Oh, Jamie! What do you want?
You know," she said playfully, "that I don't
believe in men in the kitchen."

"Barbara sent me for a match. We're out of
the fireplace kind," Jamie said. The faint soapy
smell of the dishwasher, the herby fragrance
still lingering, contributed to his sense of peace
and calm. He went back and knelt beside Barbara to light the fire, delaying the moment when
he must take up the incubus of Cannon's manuscript again.

He put his arm around her. "You are looking
awfully tired, sweetheart. Why not turn in early?"

Barbara got up wearily. Her lips were color-
less and her eyes haggard. She said, "Maybe I
will. That aspirin doesn't seem to have worked
at all; I don't remember *when* I've had such a
headache."

"Let me get you another drink," Jamie sug-

gested. He started to pour it, broke off as Dana
came in. "Would you like one, Dana?"

"If Barbara's head is really bad, she shouldn't
drink," Dana said, coming and bending over
Barbara, who now sat drooping over, her head
between her hands. "Wow, you look ghastly,
Barbara. Your face is positively *gray!*"

"See here," Jamie said, vaguely frightened,
his pleasant mood shaken. "Should I call a doctor, Barbie, or run you round to see Clifton?"

"No, no," Barbara said irritably. "I just wish
everybody would stop *fussing!* Can't I have a
headache in peace and quiet?" Her voice trembled as she tried to laugh, and she covered her
temples with her hands.

Dana's lovely face was very gentle. "You poor
thing, come on. You go in and get ready for bed,
and I'll massage the back of your neck. That's
the best thing for headaches, better than all
your pills and powders, and you'll be sleeping
like the unborn in twenty minutes. Come on."

Unprotesting, Barbara let Dana lead her out
of the room. Jamie sat by the fire, watching the
flames leap up. In fifteen minutes, Dana tiptoed
out of the bedroom and closed the door softly
behind her.

"She's fast asleep," she said.

"That was good of you, Dana," Jamie said
sincerely.

"I like doing it, but it tires me out," Dana
said. "I'll have that drink, if I may."

Jamie poured her one. He had the feeling that
she was waiting for him to say something, but
all he could think of to say was "I'm sorry to
seem unsociable, Dana. I wish I didn't have to
go over these damned manuscripts, but I do."

"Don't let me stop you; your mother and I have plenty to talk over," Dana said. She took her drink in her hand and went into Mrs. Melford's bedroom. Jamie protested, "Oh, come, you don't all have to clear out of the living room," but she had gone.

The room was quiet except for the quiet hissing and crackling of the fire. Jamie picked up the manuscript, leaving the second copy on the sideboard, wondering a little about Dana. He felt vaguely surprised that Barbara, who in the ordinary way was not jealous, should feel so harried and insecure where Dana was concerned. Dana was a sweet and pleasant girl and evidently wanted to be friendly with them both, so why couldn't Barbara accept it that way? He supposed Barbara would have felt more secure if she had been pregnant. He was in no particular hurry to have children, but he wanted them some day. Maybe I should go and see if I'm the one who's not fertile, he thought idly, and remembered, with a shudder of disgust, what the threatening voice on the telephone had said. Oh well, why worry about lunatics?

The manuscript was thick, some two hundred and fifty pages of typescript on the familiar cheap white mimeo paper that he had grown to know from Jock's earlier books, typed carefully, though not as well as a professional typist would have done it, and with the frequent x-ing out and corrections to which most professional editors quickly become accustomed. Jamie took a pencil out of his vest pocket (after twelve years as a book editor he had almost forgotten how to read without a pencil in his hand, and often absentmindedly found himself correcting typographi-

cal errors even in printed books) and began
reading.

*This is the story of a strange journey, a jour-
ney among the deluded, the mad, the obsessed—
and occasionally among those who genuinely
have strange powers: the witches of today. Not
in old castles, not in haunted Victorian houses,
but in the housing developments, the Village
apartments, right next door to you, perhaps, the
modern witch carries on his dreadful work of
black magic and evil.*

The first couple of chapters told a few com-
monplace stories of magic and voodoo, of wax-
doll murders, and Jamie thought as he read that
this sort of thing was routine enough for anyone
who had written widely in this field. Cannon
had spent his last several years researching in
the fields of psychic phenomena, haunted houses,
and the like, and if he occasionally dressed up
his information to make a "good yarn," Jamie
wasn't the one to reprove him. But toward the
end of chapter three, describing what purported
to be the operations of a modern society of black
magic masquerading as a study group of folklore and anthropology, he sat up straighter,
frowning as he read.

*My informant was formerly a member of a
black lodge, commonly miscalled a witch coven,
but after learning the depths of depravity and
horror to which the members routinely descended,
she renounced her own membership in the group.
She told me that she was trying to enter a con-
vent or, failing that, to dedicate her life to vol-*

unteer social work, to try to undo some of the dreadful things she had helped this lodge do. But four months after I met her, after a long period of fear and obsession (I admit that at first I thought she was losing her mind), she died of what the doctors called heart failure. Since she died screaming about an invisible knife piercing her heart, I have sometimes doubted the diagnosis.

Whatever the truth about the poor girl's death, it is true that she was being persecuted. She showed me the letters she had received.

Jamie shook his head distressedly. No wonder Jock had been frightened! He skipped over a brief account of how the girl had supposedly been initiated into the black lodge, of how drug addicts had been brought into the group on the promise of unlimited drugs and then, since their conscience had been partly destroyed by the drug, used for certain practices for which other members were too squeamish. Names were not mentioned, but, except for that, the book gave a remarkable circumstantial account of wickedness evidently done for its own sake.

I asked another informant, a former priest who had affiliated with the group and evidently liked the idea of publicizing their work somewhat, just why they attacked apparently innocent persons so cruelly.

"I spent my youth under the lies of religion and the fear of hellfire," he told me. "I believed that I would go to hell if I touched a woman, if I spoke disrespectfully even of the neurotic old hags of nuns who taught in my school, if I gave

*way to a moment of anger or lust; these were
supposed to be sins as terrible as murder or
torture. Now I have learned to serve a new
God—a God who makes allowances for the faults
of humanity—and I am at least learning to live.
Before I die I will have my revenge on those
who taught me that life was nothing but guilt
and fear."*

Jamie wondered if this was the "unfrocked"
Father Mansell about whom Cassidy had spoken. Unbalanced, certainly, yet evil had, must
assuredly, been perpetrated in the name of religion; those who had suffered from its most unbalanced forms might well have become themselves
mentally unbalanced. The chapter went on:

*Money, power, and the satisfaction of per-
sonal urges, however, is the usual reason given
for the activities of the black magician, and for
that reason they will stop at nothing to attain
their desires or to do away with anyone who
interferes with them. For instance, my first informant, the girl who died, told me that in three
separate cases she had sat in a circle of concen-
tration focusing all the power of the thoughts of
a dozen men and women to force a rich relative
or friend to change a will or to make over large
sums of money to a member. Whether some
form of hypnosis was employed on the victim as
well, I do not know, but it apparently worked.
The one whose will had been changed died a
few weeks later. In chapter five I tell more about
the deaths of those attacked by black magic.*

Chapter five again, Jamie flipped the pages,

skipping the interim and, his attention caught again, began to read.

There is a common principle of least action in both white and black magic, according to which material goals require material methods; nonmaterial goals, nonmaterial methods. A black lodge may contrive to kill someone by raising astral currents, but necessarily they have to lower the victim's resistance first. Every method of psychology is brought into play here, varying with the personality of the victim. They special- ize in confronting the victim with horrors hand- tailored to his psyche: obscenities for the clean- minded, blasphemies for the devout, sadistic tor- ture of animals (sometimes baptized with the name of the victim) for all but the most callous. Suggestion is the major force used, but it is unrelenting to a degree hardly believable by those who think of suggestion in the harmless terms of a repetitive advertisement on TV, admonish- ing the listener to buy a particular toothpaste. And, if the harmless methods of the advertising agency are effective, one can easily imagine how quickly and completely a victim can be broken down by this unrelenting persecution. I don't know if the powers raised are "devils" or not, but they are certainly something.

For example . . .

Jamie raised his head, listening intently. Some- where in another apartment a dog had begun barking almost hysterically. There was an odd rustling sound behind him. He turned, saw noth- ing, and scowled; was he beginning to imagine all of Jock's horrors? it vaguely occurred to him that it was nearly midnight and he was reacting like anyone else reading a horror story at night: he was getting the horrors. He bent his head to the manuscript again.

The methods of raising demons can be found in any grimoire, but as Shakespeare said, "I can call spirits from the vasty deep. / Why, so can I, and so can any man, but will they come when you do call to them?" The reason they do not come is because none but the trained black adepts have the proper method of pronouncing the "barbarous names of invocation." These names have largely been kept secret, in an oral tradition passed down from adept to adept. The technique is that used in so-called Mantra Yoga, the commonest instance being the well-known phenomenon of Caruso's high C breaking a thin wineglass. The words are declaimed, or reso-nated, not only with the entire single-minded purpose of the personality, but with the special vibration technique of highly trained voices. This does not mean loudness. It means, however, that one's whole body resonates with every syl-lable, so that it can be felt even in the palms of the hands and the soles of the feet. Without this one is in the same position as the minister at Vespers concluding, "Even so come, Lord Je-sus," at which no one in the congregation is surprised when He does not come.

Jamie jerked up his head again. A cold draft seemed to blow across his spine. Outside in the hall he heard a curious, dragging noise. Then several things happened all at once.

The telephone rang loudly. Simultaneously,

the doorbell of the apartment chimed three times in rapid succession, a swift *ding-ding-ding* that brought Jamie out of his chair in an automatic movement. He grabbed at the phone.

"Melford speaking," he snapped. "Hello?"

"Take a look outside your door," said the voice, and abruptly the phone went dead. Jamie swore, stepped rapidly toward the door, and jerked it open.

Without surprise he saw the hallway and the carpeted corridor empty. A cold draft blew up the stairs. He scowled, started to slam the door, then stopped, seeing that something was lying on the mat.

He reached down to pick it up, then, with a grimace of revulsion, let it fall. It was a small wooden cross to which had been nailed what looked like one of those plastic green frogs that small boys torment their sisters with. After a moment Jamie picked up the blasphemous thing. He was not religious, and the blasphemy did not especially trouble him, but the sick mind behind it did. He was shocked at the thought that Barbara, who was religious though not devout, might have found it first. He thought angrily of whoever had put the dead chickens on Jock's doorstep. Then, with a shudder of sick disgust, he realized that the toad on the cross was not plastic but limp and squishy. Quite obviously, it had been living a short time ago.

He had better get rid of the poor thing before Barbara or his mother saw it. He turned back into the living room and saw that Barbara, in her nightgown, had come into the room, leaving the bedroom door ajar.

"Did the doorbell wake you up, sweetheart?

Just someone playing Halloween pranks a month or so after the fact," he said, swiftly thrusting the thing behind his back.

Barbara did not answer or look at him. In fact, her eyes seemed loose, unfocused, and she moved hesitantly, without looking where she was going.

"Barbara?" he said in some fright. Had this damned business upset her as badly as all that? Was she walking in her sleep? He remembered vaguely that it was supposed to be bad for anyone to wake them up suddenly when they were sleepwalking, or was that just an old wives' tale? In any case, if she came to her senses and found herself out here, she might be frightened. He had better get her back to bed. But first he would put this filthy thing in the garbage. He thrust it through the kitchen door; he'd deal with it later. He returned to Barbara. . . .

He cried out in horror and leaped at her, just as, moving with awkward swiftness, she picked up Jock's carbon copy from the sideboard, took one swift step toward the fire, and flung the bundle of flimsy sheets into the center of the glowing coals.

"Barbara!" he yelled, no longer caring if he woke her up suddenly or not. "Are you out of your goddamned mind?"

She seemed neither to hear nor to see him. She struck his hand off her arm and moved slowly but with a dreadful purposefulness toward the easy chair where he had laid the copy he was reading—the last copy.

Jamie grabbed her arm and held on.

Barbara twisted and struggled, still not looking at him, fighting for the pages. He grabbed, twisted, thrust the copy away from her. She struggled sinuously toward it, slipping out of his hands as easily as an eel. He fought, trying to pinion both her arms, hampered by his fear of hurting her, shaking her silently. He kept repeating softly, urgently, "Barbara, wake up! Wake up! It's all right! It's all right, sweetheart! Wake up! You don't want to do that!"

Finally he wrenched the thick manuscript out of her hand, thrust it swiftly under the cushion of the chair, and with a soft "I'm sorry, darling," smacked his hand against her in a hard, openhanded slap.

Barbara gasped, shuddered, her eyes rolling, then suddenly gave a little all-over shake like a puppy coming out of water. She put her hands to her head in a bewildered gesture.

"You hit me," she gasped. "What? ... where? ..." And she began to cry.

Chapter Five

I N THE SHOCKED SILENCE—FOR A MOMENT IT SEEMED
to Jamie that he could actually *hear* the silence in the apartment—the telephone rang
again.

Barbara, still sobbing softly, started automatically toward it. Jamie said, "Don't answer it,"
and he stood gently holding her as it rang three,
four, five times, then stopped.

"Jamie, what's the *matter* with you?"

Suddenly he was angry. "What do you mean,
the matter with *me*? Are you out of your head?
Do you know what you've done?"

She shook her head slowly. "I—I don't know.
How did I get out here? Was I walking in my
sleep?"

"Are you trying to tell me you don't know?"
he retorted.

"But I don't." She was not crying, now, but
dry-eyed and incredulous, the bruise darkening
on her face. She put a hand to it automatically.

"I don't remember anything after Dana was rubbing my back. Then I was out here and you hit me."

Jamie said between clenched teeth, "You burnt up one copy of that ... that *damned* manuscript, and you did your damnedest to get at the other."

She stared at him, obviously unbelieving. "One of us is nuts," she said.

"*Somebody* is," Jamie said. He suddenly wondered why the racket hadn't waked up everyone in the apartment, then realized with some abashment that, if his mother and Dana *had* waked up to hear what sounded like Barbara and himself having a knock-down-and-drag-out fight at midnight, they would hardly come barging into it. He said, "Sweetheart, I wouldn't have hit you except I thought you were stark raving mad. You almost had the thing in the fire. Look."

He pointed at the dying coals. Barbara came and looked at the bundled black sheets that had once been the manuscript, an unburnt charred edge lying at the side of the fireplace here and there, and shook her head in horror. "I did *that*? Jamie, what's going on?"

"Nothing supernatural," he said, his anger coagulating to fury inside him, yet knowing he must cling to reason or he would start screaming and never stop. "I think this batch of psychotic freaks has started trying to break down my resistance. As for you, I suppose you got all worked up and scared after listening to Bess raving, and maybe your subconscious mind decided it would be safer not to have the manuscript around at all."

"Quite the psychologist, aren't you," Barbara
said wryly. "Do you really believe that?"

"I've got to," he said between his teeth. "But
I'll tell you one thing. I'm going to sleep the rest
of the night with this thing under my pillow.
And tomorrow morning I'm going to make a
dozen Xerox copies of it—myself. I won't even
trust my secretary with it."

He was still working at the Xerox machine
the next day, conscious that perhaps he was
being foolish and uneasily thinking of Barbara
(she had been asleep when he left, looking exhausted and sick, with her face still bruise-
darkened), when his secretary came into the back
room where he was working.

"Mr. Melford," she said primly, with a faintly
reproachful glance (which he interpreted, cor-
rectly, to mean "you shouldn't have to be doing
this kind of work"), "there's someone here to see
you."

He grumbled, "Barton about the new royalty
scale for the category fiction? tell him we can't
use more than three nurse novels a month on
that basis."

"No, it's a Mr. MacLaren."

"MacLaren," Jamie repeated, frowning. "I don't
know him."

"Shall I try to get rid of him? He said he'd
wait until you were free, in case you were busy,
but . . ."

Jamie's heart sank. He had an unpleasant pre-
monition that this was going to be more of the
lunacy that now surrounded Jock Cannon's
manuscript. He drew a page carefully away from
its backing and slid another into the machine.

"Does he look like a psycho, Martha? I've had
too much of that lately."

"Oh, no," she said quickly, surely. "He looks
nice. He reminds me a little of Father Cassidy.
Remember when the Father was in last summer
to talk about those two books? He has the same
sort of nice eyes."

"Is there anything else on my desk, Martha?"

"Well, yes, lots, but the only other thing right
now is that Roger Garth left the cover sketches
for Mrs. Wayne's new nurse novel, and Joan
Clancy's in the outer office and says she'd like to
see you for a minute."

"I'll send Garth down to the art director,"
Jamie decided. "There's no need for me to see
him. And Joan won't stay more than twenty
minutes; she never does. Send her in, and tell
this MacLaren that I'll see him next—although
if it's a manuscript you can have him leave it
with you."

He bundled up the copies of Cannon's manuscript, and, feeling slightly foolish, gave one to
Martha to put in the office safe. He put another
into his briefcase and dumped the others on his
desk. He thanked his stars that Jock was a me-
thodical old pro who always made carbons; all
too often, though contracts specified that the
publisher would get a manuscript and a carbon,
there was only one copy in existence. He supposed most people who worked in the publishing field would be relying on no more than one
copy in existence, and when they had gotten the
copy from the office and terrorized Bess—or
himself—into destroying the other, that would
be the end of the matter. But they seemed to

know he had Bess's copies. It occurred to him that perhaps he should have examined the copies carefully last night: possibly one of the copies she had turned over to him had been a first draft and somewhat different in detail from the one he had originally had here, the stolen one. Well, it was too late to worry about that now: the carbon was in the fire, and the only original typed copy around was the one he had. But it might be worth checking on the carbon in the agent's safe, just to make sure. Jock might be one of those writers, you never knew, who made first drafts and amended them substantially in revision.

At any rate, now he could turn over a copy to a copy editor and be sure that if anyone else in the office had a brainstorm, there would be a copy left. It had never happened that a printer lost a copy—though, like most editors, he had occasional nightmares about it—but it would be just his luck for it to happen this time, and he'd be *damned* if he was going to let anything go wrong now. He had his Irish up, and whoever those psychotic nuts were, they weren't going to get the better of him.

That settled, he spent a conscientious twenty minutes talking to Joan Clancy, a plump, fiftyish woman who had written detective stories, Westerns, Gothics, and even an occasional science-fiction novel, under a great variety of pen names, over the past twenty years of Blackcock Books, and had been a standby of theirs since before Jamie inherited the editorial desk. He actually enjoyed the pleasant comparative sanity of discussing whether Westerns had ended their day

and whether or not the audience that read them
had vanished completely for the TV plays. He
listened patiently, for once without mentally
twiddling his thumbs, as she dithered a little
over whether she could finish her next Gothic
before New Year's, and finally patted her on the
shoulder and ushered her out with a kindly word
or two of encouragement. Authors dropping in
could cut into a workday horribly when he was
busy, but Joan never abused the privilege, stopping by maybe three times a year and never
spending more than twenty minutes before remembering some very important shopping she
had to finish (coming to town, for her, meant
two hours by train from Long Island). So he
always made time to see her. Most of his writers
were much more casual, and he would have
hated to have the old thing feel in the way, even
though he suspected that usually she had nothing to say and simply wanted to remind him of
her existence. *As if I needed reminding, after twelve
books in five years*, he thought kindly, and wondered at the differences in people. Writers less
modest were apt to call him up after selling him
one book seven years ago and expect him to
remember not only their names but everything
they had done for his competitors since, not to
mention their latest marriage or divorce and
the names of their children or dogs!

He opened a package containing two science-
fiction novels from one of the big agencies, just
sent in by messenger, then remembered that he
had promised his secretary he would see a Mr.
MacLaren on unspecified business. *Oh well, if
the fellow wants to sell me a new Xerox or an
electric typewriter for my secretary, I can always*

steer him to the business manager, he thought
easily, and buzzed Peggy to send the man in.

He half rose to greet the newcomer. Peggy
had been right, he thought briefly: he had nice
eyes. He was a tall man, past middle age, with
neat graying hair; a high, square forehead; a big
nose and larger chin; and blue eyes, under high,
ridged graying brows, of an unusual piercing
blue, the blue that seldom survives childhood
except in Scandinavians.

"Mr. Melford? Good afternoon. It's kind of
you to see me without an appointment."

His voice was clear, pleasant, and neutral,
although Jamie felt that it could be forceful if
he were angry. He said, "That's quite all right.
What did you want to see me about?"

"Mr. Melford, I understand that your company, which has published many of the earlier
John Cannon books, is intending to publish another of the author's books posthumously."

Simultaneously Jamie's heart sank and his
temper rose. He got out of his chair and said,
"Get out!"

"I—I beg your pardon?" MacLaren said in
slight surprise.

"Go back to your psychotic friends and tell
them to go to hell. No deal. They can't scare
me."

MacLaren shook his head slightly. His eyes
were twinkling and he smiled. "Mr. Melford. I
think you are under a misapprehension."

Jamie did not sit down. He asked, "Are you
going to deny that you came here to keep up
what your friends have started, to try to get me
to withdraw Cannon's book by fair means or
foul?"

MacLaren said, "You certainly are under a misapprehension, Mr. Melford. Will you please sit down again?"

Before stopping to think, Jamie found himself back in his chair. *Have they started on me now?* he wondered, but it would have seemed churlish to get up again. He said, and knew his voice sounded surly, "Start talking. But this had better be good."

MacLaren said slowly, "I don't know what to say to you. I assume someone else has been here first and made you angry. Believe me, I am not associated with anyone else who might have contacted you. To the best of my knowledge and belief, I have never had the slightest contact with you, and I qualify it that far only because I believe I did see you once, at a distance, at a writers' convention: you were pointed out to me as the editor of Blackcock Books. I came to you, Mr. Melford, to ask if you would consider withdrawing Cannon's last book because——"

"Because you and your friends have decided you can catch more flies with honey than vinegar? Well, threats didn't work, and sweet talk won't work either."

"God protect us," MacLaren said quietly, "it's worse than I thought. Have you been threatened, Mr. Melford?"

"As if you didn't know. Look, MacLaren, I'm suspicious of anyone who asks me to withdraw that book now . . . politely or otherwise."

"I can see how you would be," the man said slowly. "It must sound like the old joke about it's spinach and the hell with it—and I can't say I blame you. But perhaps you would let me explain why I am interested in Cannon's last book."

"I think you'd better," Jamie said.

The man did not answer at once, and Jamie had a chance to notice how very still he sat, without a trace of the fidgeting that most people did, almost unconsciously, when sitting still. He asked at last, "If you knew that someone was seriously psychotic, Mr. Melford, would you give them a loaded gun? I can understand why you would want to expose these people and their rottenness. But I understand that Cannon has gone further: he has told how some of these things are done—which means that dozens of other unbalanced persons might read this book and try their hand at them."

Now Jamie was on slightly more familiar ground. He said, "Every time we've published a sex book, I've heard this same argument from phony liberals who use it as a mask for their own Puritanism, i.e., 'We can read it and be safe, but what about the poor mentally unbalanced person?' For your information, Mr. MacLaren, we publish for the general public, not for the mentally unbalanced, not for the perverted, not for the mythical average man either. I don't believe in censorship."

"Neither do I, when it's a matter of morals or such things," MacLaren said. "Just the same, I happen to believe in moral responsibility. I happen to be one of those people who think this would be a better world, for example, if the scientists who discovered the atom bomb had all been under an unbreakable oath never to reveal its uses except for peaceful purposes. Now we have the possibility that some kinds of knowledge may do as much harm as an atom bomb——"

"Oh, come now!" Jamie interrupted, almost laughing.

"Believe me, I am serious. An atom bomb kills—once. A man can only die once, and since everyone will die in this life, I personally don't think it matters whether I die alone or with nine million others, if that is God's will for me. Nor does it matter to me whether I die—or someone else dies—from a bomb or a thrown brick. I will die when my time comes, that is all. But I would do anything I could to keep any man from dying before his time, and, among other things, this book contains some information about specific ways and techniques to interfere in a man's life—and his brain."

"Would you object to a book exposing techniques for brainwashing?" Jamie asked.

"I would, if the techniques were so simple that anyone who read the book could go out and do likewise," he retorted, "as I would object to a book telling schoolchildren how to build atomic bombs in their playhouses."

Jamie shrugged. "You might be on the level and you might not," he said skeptically, "but it still sounds as if you'd decided that I couldn't be scared off but I might be talked out of it. So the answer's still no. Even if I believed that line about the dreadfully dangerous stuff in this book—which I don't—I wouldn't let myself be scared off. So go tell your friends that."

"God forbid I should speak to such people," MacLaren said with a wry smile, "but I admire your spirit. And since it is forbidden to interfere

with your free will, I can't say any more. I wish
you didn't feel this way though. Would you con-
sent, perhaps, to letting me go through the manuscript with you? You could retain as much as
you wished of the expose and sensational material, but perhaps you would be willing to delete,
or perhaps garble, the material that it is dangerous to give out."

"Nothing doing."

"Mr. Melford, you know these people are not
going to stop at threats." MacLaren said hesitantly. "I don't want to frighten you, but——"

"Let them do their damnedest! Look, get one
thing through your head: your friends——"

"THEY ARE NOT MY FRIENDS!" MacLaren
roared, so loud that he actually rocked Jamie on
his heels. Dropping his voice to normal, he said,
"I'm sorry. I shouldn't have been rude. But you
are a stubborn man, Mr. Melford, and I have a
temper. I resent your constant implication that
I am a liar and somehow allied with these people who have threatened you!"

Jamie felt his face reddening, but he persisted.
"Do you think people who tried to frighten Jock
Cannon to death and terrorize his wife—and
mine—would stop at a lie or two?"

"When you put it that way, I suppose not,"
MacLaren said. He sounded sad.

"Well then, these people, your friends or not,
can't hurt me, because I just plain don't believe
in their hogwash! Jock had started believing it,
and it was getting to him—and it might even
have killed him. But it can't get me that way,
because *I don't believe it!*" Jamie was almost
yelling now himself, and MacLaren smiled, a
sudden, wide, irresistible smile.

"That's the spirit," he said approvingly. "If you're bound and determined to take on these people single-handed, that's the only way you have a prayer of coming out of it without being damaged . . . or damned. And if you change your mind, call me. Any time. Any hour of the day or night. And I'll be praying for you."

With no further valediction he walked out of the office, leaving Jamie blinking and wondering if he had been on the level after all.

Chapter Six

BARBARA MELFORD OPENED HER EYES, FEELING
the light pierce them with dull spikes of
pain. She sat up slowly, wondering at the
silence in the apartment.

Normally the morning was full of Jamie's news
broadcast, the sounds of Mother Melford making coffee in the kitchen, water running somewhere. This morning it was completely silent
except for the heavy ticking of the clock. Barbara stared at the clock in disbelief: eleven
o'clock?

Good God,she thought, I've been sleeping like
the dead! Jamie's bed was flung back in disorder and quite empty. Then, slowly and like a
bad dream, she remembered the night before.
Had she really flung the Cannon manuscript
into the fire in a sleepwalking brainstorm? The
last thing she remembered after that was Jamie
falling asleep with the reclaimed copy under his
pillow. Then she, too, had drifted off into sleep,

uneasily wondering as she dropped off whether she might not wake again to find out that she had perpetrated some new horror.

Ill-tempered, she rose, drew on a bathrobe, and went out into the living room. Mother Melford might well be out shopping by now; maybe she would be lucky and Dana, too, would have taken herself off somewhere.

The living room was empty, but pinned to the back of a chair near the fire was a note; "Barbara, dear, you were sleeping so sweetly I hadn't the heart to wake you, and Jamie said you had had a disturbed night, so I left you to sleep. Get a good rest, dear. I'm helping Dana house-hunt. Flora Melford."

Grimacing, Barbara tossed the note into the fireplace. *I must be a thoroughly unregenerate character*, she thought. *The more she tries to be nice the more phony it seems to me, and I'm sure that's a failing in me, not her.*

Grimly, she remembered that she had two appointments this morning for photography. She called her agent and asked her to cancel them: it was too late now anyhow, thanks to Mother Melford's well-meaning kindness. A long shower made her feel better; she climbed into old jeans and a sweater, tied her damp hair up in a scarf, and padded out into the kitchen in search of some coffee to complete the cure. She stretched out her hand to the coffee canister, touched something, drew her hand back, and gasped in horror.

Stretched on the counter before her was a rough wooden cross; fastened to its surface with nails was the hideous dead body of a green frog.

Shuddering with horror, she could only stare at it, almost disbelieving.

How had it come there? If it had been there this morning—in the kitchen, of all places! —Mother Melford would have raised the roof with her screams. Barbara had no horror of dead animals as such, but the sadistic cruelty of this, and the implied blasphemy, made her feel a shiver of nausea.

Could this be some filthy joke? Mother Melford had sneered last night at her wish to bring her children up with a religious background.... Was this her further answer?

I know she doesn't like me. But she'd really have to hate me to do a thing like that.

And would any sane person torture a poor defenseless animal, just for a—a dirty joke on me?

Barbara was not naive and she knew that animal torture was not unheard-of, but finding it coming this close was unnerving. She started to pick the thing up and put it into the incinerator, then hesitated as it hit her like a ton of bricks: *This is the sort of thing they did to Jock Cannon.*

Now they've started on me.

But why me? Why not Jamie? Had I better save this to show him?

No, it would only upset him worse....

But she found, when she stretched out her hand again to pick up the thing, that her fingers would not receive it. After a moment she left it there, made herself a cup of instant coffee from the hot-water faucet, and went into the living room to drink it so that she would not have to see the damnable thing.

All right. So whoever tried to scare Jock silly has started their damned war of nerves on us.

But how did it get *into* the apartment? Has someone been able to come in here while I slept? That would mean someone has a duplicate key.

She had only glanced through Jock Cannon's earlier books, but now, impelled by a vague half-memory, she went and found an old copy of *The Devil in America* and riffled through it quickly. Amid an account of chicken sacrifices in New Orleans voodoo rites, she found the following:

> *The late Aleister Crowley left an account of a bizarre ceremony in which a toad, baptized Jesus, son of Joseph, was kept for three days in an ark of cedar wood, with incense burnt before him, prayer, and worship. Meanwhile, the magician would carve a cross and on the third day crucify the animal.*

But Jock's book gave no hint of *why* anyone would perform such a pointless piece of nastiness and blasphemy. Barbara herself had always supposed that such things were the acts of people who, having for some good reason left the church, wished to kick and publicly scorn what they had once worshiped. Seeing it at close hand, however, she had a queasy sense of having touched lunacy.

She thought dully, *I ought to get rid of it before Jamie comes home,* but she remained sitting in the chair as if paralyzed, the book fallen laxly in her hand. In the ashes of last night's fire she saw undisturbed black flakes, close together: the manuscript that had been burnt.

How could I do a thing like that? I've never walked in my sleep, not even when I was a little girl.

Steps and voices in the hall roused her slightly from her lassitude, and when Mrs. Melford came in with Dana, both smiling and brisk from the outside air, she was sitting up finishing her coffee.

"Hello, Barbara dear." The older woman came over to kiss her. "How is your headache? Has Jamie called? Didn't you go to the office today?"

"Of course I did," Barbara said a little wryly. "This is just my astral body you're seeing. Hello, Dana. Did you have any luck house-hunting?"

"I looked at one place, and I'll probably take it," Dana said. "Are you feeling better, Barbara? You don't look at all well, and Jamie said you'd walked in your sleep."

The thought of the three of them discussing her at breakfast was distasteful. Barbara said dryly, "I'm quite well, thank you," and stood up, the book trailing from her hand.

"What are you reading? Oh"—Mrs. Melford made a grimace of distaste—"*that* thing!" She picked up her shopping bag. "I suppose I'd better get some lunch . . ."

She walked through the kitchen doors and the next moment recoiled through them again with a shrill scream. "Oh! Oh! Oh. . . ."

Barbara flinched. She had left the ghastly crucified toad lying on the kitchen cupboard close to the coffee canister.

The older woman, her face distorted and agitated, turned on Barbara with a cry. "Did you put that there? Did you leave it there? It's horrible. Oh! Oh! I can't touch it."

Barbara went toward the kitchen wearily. She said, "I'm sorry. I should have put it into the incinerator, but I thought Jamie should see it, so I left it there . . ."

"*You* left it there? Are you crazy, you leaving such a thing . . ."

"I mean, I *found* it there," Barbara said wearily, "and I didn't move it again."

"But Barbara," Dana said, her sweet bewildered face blank and her eyes enormous, "how could you *find* it there? It wasn't there when we ate breakfast, was it, Mother?"

Mrs. Melford said vigorously, "It certainly was *not*! And it didn't walk there on its own feet! And no one's been here but *you*, Barbara! Are you playing some joke? It's not very funny, but——"

"I didn't," Barbara protested, "and I don't think it's funny either. I went out about half an hour ago to get some coffee and it was lying there. I—I couldn't touch it," she finished weakly.

Mrs. Melford regarded her skeptically. Dana frowned a little, her clear blue eyes regarding Barbara in distress and dismay. "But Barbara, if no one else has been here, are you *sure* you didn't put it there . . . maybe walking in your sleep?"

"I haven't walked in my sleep but that once," Barbara said, feeling suddenly trapped and angry, "and I *didn't*. Maybe *you* put it there."

Dana didn't even answer that. She shrugged eloquently and turned away, saying to Mrs. Melford, "I think she's not feeling very well, Mother. Don't bother her."

Barbara shook her head, wondering if she were really a lunatic being humored, as Mrs. Melford said in a careful undertone, "Her brother—poor Jerry—somehow I feel to blame. I wouldn't want that to happen again . . ."

She came back, carrying the dead frog on the

cross in her hand. *For all her shrieks,* Barbara thought with some detachment, *she seems to handle it without any qualms.*

"Why don't you come and lie down again, Barbara, and I'll bring you some lunch when it's ready," Dana said, stretching out her hand. Barbara felt trapped and irritable. She said, "I'm all right now."

"Well, you don't act it. I'll put this in the incinerator," said Mrs. Melford, and she went out into the hall, heading toward the incinerator shaft. Dana said in an undertone, "She's only worrying about you, Barbara. Don't be cross."

"I'm not cross. And to prove I'm thinking well of her," Barbara said a little grimly, "I'll save her some work by going and making my own bed and doing our room myself, since I'm not at the office."

"Oh, does she do all your housework? You lucky thing, you," Dana said with wide eyes. "Do you know what cleaning women cost?"

"Yes," Barbara said tersely, "I've tried often enough to hire them; I have no intention of making a household drudge out of my husband's mother. But she simply refuses to have anyone else in the apartment. They would get under her feet, she says."

"No one accused you of it," Dana said. "Goodness, you're touchy this morning! What are you reading?" She took Barbara's hand, still holding the book, in hers. She turned it over to look at the garish cover. "Ugh! No wonder you're feeling morbid!"

Barbara made a determined effort. Freeing her hand from the soft pressure of Dana's, she

said, "Don't mind me; I'm not fit to talk to. I'll
go and do my room. No, I don't want any lunch,
not right now anyhow; later today I have to
drop in at the office and I'll get a bite downtown. I don't mean to sound touchy, Dana." She
walked into her room and shut the door, putting
her hands to her head.

*Dana means well, too, I suppose, but that sweet,
wide-eyed look of hers is just too damn much!
Nobody can be that sweet!*

Grimly, she spread up her bed and Jamie's,
mopped out the bath and shower, brushed the
floor—a lick and a promise—with a dust mop.
Inside she was seething a little. She would much
rather have hired a cleaning woman. Jamie's
mother kept insisting that a strange woman in
the house meddling with all their things would
just be an invasion of privacy. *But she never
stops to think that being here at all invades Jamie's
privacy and mine.*

At first Barbara had had a pronounced distaste for Jamie's mother making their beds, possibly rummaging through her bureau drawers,
handling her lingerie, her comb and brush. She
had tried to make a point of doing her own
room. But Mrs. Melford had been absolutely
hurt—and sarcastic. "You think I am going to
snoop in your bureau drawers maybe? Look in
your private papers? Rummage in your medicine cabinet maybe, to see what pills you take?"

"No, no," Barbara had tried to protest, feeling
guilty because that was exactly what she felt, "I
just don't like to treat you like a servant. . . ."

"A servant? A servant? You come from a family that has servants? I am not so high-toned, I
only want to be like in my own house. I like to

work!" Then her voice had drooped: "But me, I
am only a poor old grandma, not a lady of the
house with her own kitchen anymore. I would
be better in the old ladies' home! I thought for a
little while I could be at home. . . ."

"Oh, for God's sake, Mother!" Barbara had
protested. "Do whatever you want to!"

"And have you suspect me? No, I tell you
what you should do!" A sad, malevolent smile
had come over the old woman's face. "All your
secrets, all the things you don't want me to
see—you get a big lock, lock them all up. . . ."

"Oh, good grief, Mother, I haven't any *secrets*!"
Barbara almost shouted, feeling like a rebel-
lious teenager, guilty and distressed. "I'm *sorry*!
If you can't understand what I meant, just forget it! Forget it!"

And Jamie had said, half in apology, "Mother's always had her own house to keep and I
guess she feels lonesome unless she's doing housework. She's not what you'd call intellectual, you
know."

That seemed true. The old woman read little,
never watched television, seemed to dislike the
radio, and had no hobbies except the small herb
garden she grew chives and sage in for flavoring
food, tarragon in flowerpots, sweet basil, and
half a dozen other little flowerpots that Barbara
didn't recognize but which smelled generally
pleasant, sweet or pungent or bitter, and whose
taste she usually recognized in some stew or
roast . . . the old lady was an expert cook.

Nor did she seem to have many friends, except for the immediate way she had taken to
Dana. In a younger woman, Barbara would have
wondered if Jamie's mother had Lesbian tend-

encies; their sudden friendship was almost like a crush.

But now, as Barbara glumly swept, dusted, and mopped, she found that the physical effort was restoring her good humor somewhat. *After all*, she thought, *the poor old thing is lonely. She can't seem to like me, so maybe it's nice to have a young friend whom she can treat as a daughter. And if Dana cared about Jamie, I ought to be sorry for her instead of feeling catty and mean. Anyhow, I shouldn't begrudge Mother Melford a friend or two; goodness knows, I have plenty of friends. She could be filling up the apartment with a whole crew of old hags her own age. I've been spared that, anyway.*

But that crack about Jerry. Did she mean that I might be going the same way?

Isn't sleepwalking supposed to be a sign of mental disturbance?

She had never done such a thing before. A psychologist had told her once that she was almost sickeningly free of neurotic tendencies: "If everybody was like you, Barbara, I'd be out of a job," he had laughed. Barbara herself had simply wondered if the trouble was a lack of imagination.

"Well, I'm making up for it now," she said half-aloud, and went to put the dust mop away.

Could Mother Melford have played such a cruel trick with the dead animal?

Jamie would certainly never do such a thing. And yet, if the apartment had been locked, and no one else had been inside . . .

Barbara told herself not to be paranoid. But there were only five possibilities. One: Mother Melford or Dana had left it there for her. But why would they do such a thing?

Two: Jamie had left it there for her. No. She knew Jamie, and damn it, he *wouldn't*. Not even by oversight would he have left it where she, or his mother, or even Dana, could have found it.

Three: someone had a key to the apartment. That was certainly the most likely possibility, but still improbable. This war of nerves had commenced only a day or two ago; could they have armed themselves like this *already*?

Four: the animal had materialized like something at a spiritualist séance. That was too ridiculous to be considered for a moment. She was willing to believe in murder by suggestion and fear, but not by gross outrage of natural law and common sense.

Five: she herself, sleepwalking or in a fit of insanity, had done it. Barbara was seized with sudden terror. She had burned the manuscript —at least, Jamie told her she had, and she had seen its charred flakes. What else might she have done?

She lay down, stretched out on her bed, and tried vainly to think back to last night. The ghastly headache. Dana offering to rub her neck. She had no memory of undressing or getting into bed, but only of blinding pain that slowly, slowly subsided under the almost hypnotic touch of Dana's hands, slowly stroking back and forth along her neck as if drawing the pain out along an electric wire. Dana's soft, soothing voice.

She's so nice to me and I'm so nasty about her.

Jamie should have married her. She's much nicer than I am.

Hey, did she hypnotize me?

I am getting paranoid! Dana wouldn't do a thing like that.

Dimly Barbara realized that she had work to do, that she should get up and dress, telephone her agent again and ask about afternoon appointments, call the beauty shop for an appointment—she needed her hair trimmed and set, look in the paper to see if the January white sales were predicted yet—they needed some towels, and perhaps shop for Christmas presents. Would Dana be with them for Christmas? What could she get her for a present? But she still felt too weary to deal with any of these things.

Out in the other room Dana had turned on the radio—no, she was singing. Her voice was low and tuneless, like a wind, and the song seemed to go on and on, in repeated fragments. Barbara yawned; it had a drowsy sound. But good heavens, after sleeping almost till noon, she could hardly take a nap at two in the afternoon!

She picked up *The Devil in America,* opened it at random, and began to read again.

While these white witches have no contact with the devil or with any Satanist society, and attribute their powers to beneficial natural law, they seem to be allied in legend to the midwife, sage-femme—which means, simply, wise woman—on the grannekener of old Norse, surviving as the "granny woman" in the Appalachian mountains. Love charms, charms for "removing crossed conditions," and charms to enable the barren to bear children, are their stock in trade.

Maybe that's what I need, Barbara thought sleepily—*a fertility charm. One of those old fertility cults, with orgies, might have a vogue, at that, down in the East Village where the hippies congregate. I guess anyone who wants to hold orgies doesn't really need a fertility cult.*

She read on, forcing her eyes to focus: *you can't be sleepy at this hour.*

Quite the reverse of the well-meant, though probably useless, love charms of the white witch are the malevolent charms, hex-bags, and curse paraphernalia of the black witch or sorceress. I have seen charms to bring impotence upon men, to destroy marriages, to bring sterility to women. The power of suggestion is strong, but I do not discount the possibility of telepathic power even where the cursed one supposedly does not know of the curse.

The book fell from Barbara's hand. *Rubbish,* she thought drowsily. *Poor Jock, he believed all this stuff and they scared him to death with it.* She closed her eyes.

Just a little nap. . . .

Dana's voice in the other room, like clear running water, went on and on, and Barbara gradually slipped beneath the surface of the water, which went on rippling over her head.

She seemed to be in a great, gray-vaulted hall, with pillars all round, reflecting black gleams as if they were made of ebony or of polished jet. In the middle of the great hall a fire burned, smoldering, with a sweet scent that had an overtone of bitterness. Barbara found herself walking toward the fire on wavering legs, as if she were walking under water.

A dark figure squatted over the fire, hands protruding white and bony beneath the flowing

black-hooded robe. Between the hands Barbara
saw the limp form of some small animal, a mouse
or small cat, a knife. . . . The soft toneless chant
rose to a hypnotic rhythm of chanting, a knife
flashed, there was a strange small cry. . . .

Hearing herself whimper aloud, Barbara drew
herself upright with an almost convulsed start.
The room was empty, her familiar bedroom.
There was no hall, no pillars, no shrouded figure, no dead animal. . . .

Her hand, lying on the bed at her side, contracted in horror. Warm and limp at her side,
something . . . *something* . . .

She turned frantic eyes. It was there, still
warm, the throat still trickling red blood: a large
gray mouse, quite dead and not yet cold.

A scream contracted Barbara's throat but never
escaped. Dana was still singing her fragmentary
melody in the other room, and she could smell
the good smell of roasted meat with herbs in
the kitchen. The other women were innocently
employed around the apartment, and she . . .
she

What had she done?

Could one of them have come into the room
without Barbara hearing?

If she called out to them now . . .

If she accused them . . .

If they denied it, what could she say? Already
Mother Melford thought she was going the way
of her brother—quite insane.

Had she gotten up in her sleep, somehow
caught a mouse, killed it in her sleep?

That was—that was insane! She *couldn't*!

Had one of the women (they hated her, they
must hate her!) played this as a filthy trick? And

if she accused them, who in the world would believe that any apparently sane woman would have done such a thing?

She clutched at vanishing sanity. Why would they do such a thing? Surely they didn't hate her. They were kind to her. Mother Melford voluntarily did all her housework, freeing Barbara to work without the frantic drudging of most working housewives. Dana had tried to help her headache. Was she, Barbara, losing her mind like poor Jerry?

She knew that thinking one's self the victim of a plot was often the first sign of insanity.

But was it better to believe one was the victim of a plot, or to believe that she herself had lost her mind, walked in her sleep, and added mouse-killing to book-burning? She clutched at her head with both hands and said aloud, "God help me!"

There was the dead mouse, horribly limp and now beginning to stiffen. There was blood on the blanket. With an almost feverish revulsion, Barbara went into her bathroom and wrapped the dead animal in a Kleenex.

Jamie will never believe this. I ought to keep it and show it to him.

Then will he think I'm crazy?

The whole room seemed somehow throbbing. Barbara sat down at her dressing table, waiting for the pounding to subside.

Blood on the bed . . . spilled blood.

Blood . . .

She headed for the bathroom again in a hurried stride, where she promptly lost the cup of coffee that was all she had consumed since the previous night. Long after it had come up she still bent over the bowl, retching sickly, her whole body aching with the violence of sickness. Finally she washed her face in cold water, went and lay down again on the bed, and sprang up again as if galvanized, unable to endure the touch of slick wet blood.

In a nervous frenzy she stripped the bed of blankets and sheets, stuffing the soiled sheets into the hamper with almost guilty haste.

Mother Melford will see the blood on the sheets. What will she think?

She'll probably think I'm having my period and that I've been careless, that's all. Humiliating as that thought was, it was better than the truth.

Who would have thought one small mouse could have bled so much? It seemed to Barbara that the foul-smelling blood had penetrated blankets, sheets, mattress pad, even stained the mattress. There was a curious, sick, dusty smell in the air, like—like a nest of mice, she thought with revulsion. Are there—*could* there—be mice in the mattress?

Tugging, her hands trembling, she pulled the mattress half off the bed, looking for any signs of gnawing or nibbling. The mattress seemed intact, but the evil smell now seemed to pour out in waves, almost overcoming her with nausea. She squeezed between the bed and the wall, pushing the last side of the mattress away. The mattress overbalanced and toppled to the floor, leaving the box spring bare, in its green and white ticking. Lying in the middle of it, pressed down by the spring, was a small coarse-cloth bag.

As if in a dream, Barbara reached for it.

What is this? I didn't put it here.

But then, when was the last time I made the bed? Mother does all the work in the apartment.

Jamie's mother. But why would she put anything in my bed?

Slowly, her fingers almost refusing to hold it, she picked up the small linen bag.

It was made of coarse natural linen, the dull yellowed flax color of the unbleached cloth. It was tied at the top with a coarse black string, knotted with a series of intricate knots. Barbara struggled with them for a few minutes stubbornly, then reached over to her dressing table, picked up her nail scissors and cut them.

The bag had a strange, sickish, musty smell. *Mother Melford's herb garden. But those are sweet herbs: they smell nice! I know some people buy lavender for sachets, but nobody in his right mind would put this stuff in a sachet: it stinks.*

She pulled at the cut strings and tipped the contents out into her hand.

There was a curious, shriveled black bean. There was a lock of hair: incredulously, Barbara recognized it as her own, coiled into a tiny braid and knotted. There were two small, wrinkled black objects that smelled and were obviously of animal origin, and Barbara realized she did not want to think of what they were. There were two grains of what looked like rye or wheat, smudged with some filthy black stuff that stank. There was a small black piece of parchment with words written on it in ink, but the handwriting was so sprawling that Barbara could not even make out the letters, though she had the vague impression that it was not in English. There was one thing more in the bag, but it stuck there, and Barbara, working it out slowly with shaking fingers, felt sick again. What was this, anyhow?

The book she had just been reading had mentioned fertility charms. Had Mother Melford gotten impatient with Barbara's slowness at having children and put some sort of fertility charm in her bed? Numbly, hardly knowing what she did, Barbara thought, *Well, that's the right place for it.*

She wedged the last item out of the bag. It was a piece of stiff cardboard. Turning it over, Barbara discovered that a snapshot of herself, taken with her own small camera, had been pasted on the cardboard. She stood there in a bathing suit, her hair wet and flopping, poised on a diving board.

But there was a mark on the figure. Her fingers suddenly trembling, Barbara raised it toward her face.

The breasts of the figure had been slashed with a razor blade. And the belly of the photograph had been burnt through with something like a cigarette.

Barbara let the photograph drop from her lax fingers. She could not control her shaking. She felt like screaming. No fertility charm this! But sterility? Death? She felt sudden overwhelming revulsion. She gagged again, feeling sourness in her mouth.

Who? Why?

There was a soft knock on the door. Dana called quietly, "Barbara? Do you want some lunch?"

I won't answer, Barbara thought, frantic as a trapped animal. *She'll think I'm still asleep. She'll go away.*

"Barbara? Dear?"

Still Barbara did not answer. The knob of the door turned and Dana came in.

Barbara had just presence of mind to knock the small bag to the floor. *She thought I was asleep and she came in anyhow.*

Maybe she put the mouse there.

"Why, Barbara, I thought you were asleep," Dana exclaimed. Her eyes widened when she saw Barbara still standing between the bed and the wall, the mattress and all the blankets on the floor. "Why, what on earth are you doing?"

"Just making up the bed," Barbara replied, her voice not steady, but holding the muscles of her face with rigid control.

For now she knew the truth—or rather, truth had one of two faces, and both were masks of terror.

Either she was insane . . .

. . . or she was surrounded, in her own house, by vicious and insane enemies.

Chapter Seven

IT WAS ALREADY GREYING TOWARD DUSK WHEN
James Melford said good night to his secretary, took his fur cap from the rack, and let
himself out the front door of Blackcock Books.
Going down in the elevator, he thought with
some relief that Cannon's controversial book—
his *most* controversial book, he amended, for
Jock's earlier books had raised some controversy,
mostly as to whether Blackcock Books should
have gone into this field of publishing at all—
was now safely in the hands of a copy editor
and that extra copies were in the office safe and
in his briefcase. Short of an all-out attack on
copy editor, office, and possibly the printer, the
unknown factors who were trying to prevent the
publication of the book might just as well stop
wasting their breath.

He felt a sort of euphoria. If the unknowns,
whoever or whatever they might be, had sent
MacLaren to his office to find out how he was

standing up under their war of nerves, he flat-
tered himself that he'd sent MacLaren away un-
satisfied. By now it was a personal contest
between himself and these lunatics, and he wasn't
going to let them get any satisfaction.

He paused on the way out of the building,
then crossed the street, went into the public
library, and stopped to consult the telephone
books for the five boroughs.

He already knew that Manhattan would yield
nothing; the Bronx and Staten Island were
equally barren of Walters in the family of
Mansell. The Queens phone book listed a Walter
M. Mansell, but when Jamie stepped into a pay
phone booth, dialed the number, and asked if a
Father Mansell lived there, the childish voice
that answered said "What?" so blankly that
Jamie said hastily, "Sorry, wrong number," and
hung up in confusion. An unfrocked priest might
conceivably marry but would hardly have young
children—he had heard a background of childish voices playing some noisy game—old enough
to answer the telephone.

He was about to leave the booth in disgust
when he remembered that there was one bor-
ough remaining. The Brooklyn phone book yielded
a Walter Mansell, and when he dialed the number, a strong bass voice answered, "Yes?"

Jamie found himself momentarily speechless.
Now that he had probably chased Father Mansell
to earth he didn't know what to say to him.
Finally he said, stumbling a little, "I—I beg
your pardon, I am not sure I have the right
Mansell. Is this the Walter Mansell who used"
—*Oh God*, he thought, *I can't say "who used to*

be a priest—" "who used to know John Cannon, the writer?"

The bass voice sounded faintly puzzled. "Why, yes, I know Cannon. What can I do for you?"

"It's a little complicated," Jamie said slowly. "I take it you know that Cannon is dead?"

Now there was no mistaking the shock and horror in Mansell's voice. "Dead? No, I—when did this happen? When was he killed?"

"Killed." It flashed through Jamie's mind that if he put it this way, Mansell had almost been expecting the news. Surely the normal question on hearing of a death was "How did he die?" Jamie said, on a quick impulse, "Yes, they got him."

"'Filthy devils!" Mansell said sharply. "But who are you?"

Jamie explained, adding, "Jock said your name just a short while before he died. It was a heart attack evidently."

Mansell's voice sounded cautious now. "But you said *they got him.*"

Jamie made up his mind. "I think I have to talk to you, F—er—Mr. Mansell. When could I see you?"

"I suppose I must go to Cannon's funeral," said the stranger in a hesitant voice. "I don't know. I would rather not have you come here. If you are who you seem to be, you'll know why. Where are you calling from?"

"I'm at the public library, as a matter of fact."

"In Manhattan? Well, look. Suppose I meet you there. I can hop on a subway and be there in twenty minutes," Mansell said. "I don't wear a Roman collar anymore; I suppose you know. How will I recognize you?"

Jamie chuckled. "I'm damned if I'll go out and get a white carnation for my buttonhole at this hour. I'm carrying a briefcase and wearing a fur cap."

The bass voice snorted a little. "I'll find you somehow."

Jamie went into the reading room and spent fifteen minutes looking through an issue of *Time* magazine, several weeks old, without paying much attention to it. Somewhere in the back of the book a word jarred his senses, and he read with some attention the account of a self-styled minister of something calling itself the First Satanic Church of America who had performed a black nuptial mass for a couple of crazies in California. The bride had worn crimson, the altar had been a naked woman, and the minister had delivered a homily on how Satanism was really the religion of enjoying life, as witnessed by the fact that their altar was not a dead stone and puritanical clothing, but naked and alive. Jamie shook his head a little. A week ago he would have had nothing but laughter at the thought of such nonsensical friskiness; now he wondered if this lighthearted jollification was the work of the naive who had read too many books—or whether it masked something more sinister. After all, if you wanted to be free to do the devil's work in peace, wouldn't it be best to have people laughing at Satanism as nonsense for people with more time and money than brains?

With a start he realized that it was time to meet Mansell.

He went out into the lobby and watched people coming and going. It was quite dark now, and in the square before the library, crowds of men, women, and children, laden with Christmas-shopping packages, hurried here and there on obvious errands. Teen-age boys and girls, in school uniforms and laden with books, went up the library steps, and other groups came down. Across the street in front of a large department store, a Salvation Army worker monotonously jangled a bell.

Jamie had not been waiting more than seven or eight minutes when a large burly man came slowly up the steps and directly to where he was standing.

"Melford?" he asked. "I'm Mansell. We can't talk in the library. Where can we go?"

"There's a Child's across the street," Jamie said. "We can get a drink there if you like."

"Just coffee for me, thanks," the man said. "Yes, I suppose that will do as well as anything else." He was tall and burly, with heavy jowls shadowed with dark stubble, and dark eyes, rather small. For all his size there was something about him that made Jamie think incongruously of a bird, and then he realized what it was: the small, continuous, almost imperceptible head and eye movements, as if Mansell were looking all round him at once, all the time.

"Shall we go? No, wait a minute." The big man drew suddenly back into the shadow of the vestibule, almost colliding with someone coming out. Jamie looked around curiously and Mansell said, "No, I guess it's all right. I thought I saw—" He broke off and, jerking his head toward Jamie to follow, plunged into the crowded inersection. Jamie, following as best he could at Mansell's heels, thought, with irritation, that this newcomer was as crazy as everyone else he'd met in connection with this business.

Inside the restaurant Mansell placed himself, with some care, where he could see the door, craning past Jamie quite obviously with his head and those quick nervous movements. His eyes kept up the bird analogy; they were bright almost to the point of glittering. Jamie ordered coffee and Mansell ordered the same. Then, abruptly changing his mind, Mansell asked for hot chocolate. Jamie would rather have had a drink, but he wanted his wits about him just in case.

"Now tell me." Mansell's voice was deep and strong and resonant, as if accustomed to being obeyed. "How did Cannon die? And what prompted you to get in touch with me?"

"As I told you, he said your name just a few minutes before he died. From the way he spoke I thought you were a priest."

The tight mouth barely moved in a smile. "I was . . . once."

"And now you're mixed up with . . . Satanists . . . or whatever they are?"

"You don't know?" Mansell stared straight at him, a most disconcerting gaze.

"I only know that Cannon was afraid of them."

The big man drew a long, deep breath. "I don't quite understand how you come into this. Cannon never mentioned you. And I've never seen—" He stopped and scowled, broke off, half rose, craning his head over the other tables.

Jamie asked in some irritation, "Are you expecting someone to join you here?"

Mansell picked up his chocolate and drank it almost all at a gulp, greedily. He said, "If you

know how John Cannon died, you'll know why
I'm . . . shaken up."

"I only know that someone was frightening
Jock out of his wits," Jamie said angrily, "and
trying to scare his wife, and then trying to scare
me."

"And you're publishing anyhow?"

Jamie tried to remember if he had said anything about being Jock's publisher. Oh, yes, he
must have on the phone. He said, "I'm publishing anyhow. But we have one thing in common:
I don't know where *you* come into this."

"Cannon didn't tell you?"

"He didn't have a chance."

Mansell did that looking-round act again. He
said, "You have read his book?"

"More or less." Jamie drank some coffee, wondering if the man was drunk or not quite all
there. He kept acting as if he were going to say
something important and then not saying it.
And yet, if Jock had wanted to see him just
before he died . . .

Mansell signaled to the waitress to refill his
cup. He stirred it round and round, making
creamy swirls in the dark surface. Then he said,
slowly and broodingly, "When I left the church,
I was—like most of us—bitter . . . angry. I found
work as a librarian, and sort of . . . pulled the
hole in after me and disappeared. Then . . . someone approached me, obviously looking for an
ex-priest. I hardly know how to explain this; I
wasn't attempting deliberate blasphemy, I was
simply . . . curious." His voice was warm and
resonant; he leaned forward a little toward Jamie,
too tense to smile but obviously trying to. "I

don't know how to explain this—are you by any
chance a Catholic?"

"No."

"Then you won't really understand, but I'll
try. When you're a priest, you don't—I hardly
know how to explain, it would be easier if you
were Catholic—there are things you just don't
do ... or even think about doing. Books you
don't read. Paths you simply never examine.
Things you never try. Especially when, like me,
you go straight from a parochial school to the
fathers' school to seminary to the priesthood. My
life all mapped out. A sort of brainwashing. I
felt my life had been squeezed dry—all the life
out of it. I really had no intention of going out
and committing all the deadly sins one after
another; I just wanted to see what some of these
things were all about ... what people meant
when they talked about ... certain things." He
sounded almost fierce. "Just for once, I wanted
to investigate on my own instead of reading
what ten thousand church fathers had said about
it three hundred years before I was born!"

"I think I can understand that well enough."

"Right. It was a sort of adolescent rebellion,
only it was coming thirty years too late." He
broke off, sounding fierce again. "Just by any
chance, are you going to ask me to get you into
them somehow?"

"God forbid!" Jamie said, honestly shocked.
"I thought I made it clear which side I was on!"

And he wondered, after he asked: was there
room still for question in his mind about which
side *Mansell* was on?

Mansell's head darted around Jamie's to look
quickly at the door and darted quickly back. He

said, "Excuse me just a minute. I want to check something."

He got up from the table, leaving Jamie sitting there startled, went toward the back, and disappeared into the men's room, or so Jamie imagined; there was hardly anywhere else he would have gone. He was gone a considerable time, during which Jamie had begun to wonder if the man had ducked out and left him, but at last the big burly form thrust itself back toward the table and slid into the seat.

"Sorry to keep you waiting. I had to check—well, I was going to tell you how I got into this. At first it was curiosity; I went along with them, let them show me things and tell me things. It seemed—at first—a sort of rather childish craziness, adolescent dirtiness if you like ... like a gang of kids getting together to smoke marijuana and maybe getting one of the girls to take off her clothes, you see? Nasty maybe, by some viewpoints naughty ... but somehow not *serious*. I thought at first it was a sort of lunatic game, playing at blasphemy."

"It seems an odd game to join in, though," Jamie said.

"As I said, it began as a sort of adolescent rebellion for me," he repeated; and Jamie, remembering what he had read about the Satanist wedding in California, said, "And it was more than that?"

"It was more than that," Mansell said bleakly. "And now—I am damned."

"Oh, come," Jamie protested, suddenly feeling that this whole thing was too intense, "you can't believe that—not really! Do you really believe that God takes account of what foolish things people do?"

"I am damned," Mansell repeated slowly, and his bright eyes looked suddenly dull and almost glazed; again Jamie found himself wondering if the man was drunk. "And they——"

"What just a minute," Jamie said. "Who are *they*, anyhow? Everybody is too damned vague for my taste. These people can't all be just witches and hobgoblins, 'old Uncle Tom Cobbleigh and all'! They didn't come inside Dracula's coffin from Transylvania! They must have names and addresses and even, heaven help us, telephone numbers and means of livelihood; it seems unlikely that they'd be able to make much of a living at calling up demons. It's not much of a profession these days. And even the medieval alchemists never managed to spin straw into gold. So before you start talking about what 'they' did, why not start out by telling me who and what 'they' are?"

Mansell whistled softly. "Fools rush in where angels fear to tread," he said. "The last man who had any names and addresses didn't live long enough to make good use of that knowledge. Do you mean you'd take the risk?"

"I've still got to be convinced that there is any risk," Jamie said, and Mansell looked at him, owl-eyed, and then, surprisingly, grinned . . . a tipsy sort of grin. Jamie became more and more convinced that he had sneaked off for a drink—or maybe a dose of some drug, though his pupils didn't seem contracted: he wasn't on heroin. Or was it dilated that they were supposed to be? Jamie wished he had a better memory. Mansell's birdlike eyes now looked wide and lax, like black pools of ink. "You poor sucker," Mansell said, "all guts and no brains. Look here!" He banged softly on the table and the empty cocoa cup rattled. "Do you know what they do to someone who gets into their group—takes the oaths—then tries to get out again? You've read Jock's book?"

"Mumbo jumbo. Suggestion."

"Listen!" Mansell said harshly, his voice kept pitched low, yet vibrating so violently that again the cup rattled in the saucer. "First they broke down her resistance. They found out what her pet nightmares were—and made them come alive. Are you afraid of rats?" he demanded suddenly.

"A little. Anyone who's been overseas—I was in Korea."

"How would you like to wake up—out of a sound sleep—and find your bed, your nice, clean, comfortable bed, filled with live rats?"

Jamie shuddered and made a face.

"Ah, yes. Only the beginning. Suppose you woke up and found you couldn't move hand or foot and the rats were running over you? Suppose when you ordered dinner in a restaurant the waiter put a dead rat on your plate—and when you screamed and made a scene and looked again, it was a cheese omelet with pancakes? Suppose your room smelled sickly with the stench of the creatures and whenever you closed your eyes you heard them running and squeaking in the walls?"

"I guess I'd think someone was trying to break down my nerve," Jamie said.

"Suppose you had nightmare after nightmare where you were trapped in dens full of rats? Listen!" Mansell said again, and paused. So compelling was the pause that Jamie cocked his head, suddenly wondering if he would hear, in that silence, the squeak of a rat.

"Once demoralized, the fun starts," Mansell said fiercely between his teeth. "I was part of it. Imagine, if you will, thirteen men and women—the coven—sitting in the magic circle for thirteen hours. Naked. Painted with symbols. No water, no food, only the black incense burning, and concentrating. Concentrating. Concentrating. Do you know the power of a thought? You know that if someone is watching you steadily, you will feel it—feel it and be uneasy? That is a little, tiny game of thought power. Imagine thirteen trained minds—trained with years of work. Not hampered by even the slightest remnant of goodwill or inhibitions. Sitting motionless for thirteen hours—just imagine how much training *that* would take, all by itself—and willing her to death, willing her to every agony the human mind and body can experience. . . ."

His voice trailed off. His glittering eyes held Jamie's spellbound. Finally he made a slight, dismissing movement, and Jamie stirred uncomfortably and picked up his coffee. It was cold.

He said, "It sounds as if you're trying to scare me."

"You're blinking right I'm trying to scare you," said the ex-priest. "Look! I don't come out of this sounding like a hero—you're getting ready to ask me why I went along with it . . . damned myself."

"As a matter of fact, I wasn't. But why *did* you?"

"Scared," Mansell said laconically. "If they could do it to her, they could do it to *me*. I suppose I spent all my ... nerve, all my emotional force, on the hassle when I left the church. I sat there and watched the others hating and found myself hating with them. I wanted—maybe you won't be able to understand this—nothing else in life but to get out of that filthy room and away from that blonde woman with the face of a saint and the devil's eyes, and yet, at the same time—oh, there's power in it," he said softly. "I've known what it is to bring God down to man, and now I was seeing the other side ... to bring man down ... a sort of Godness too...."

"It sounds like rubbish," said Jamie forthrightly, and Mansell, the flow of his narrative interrupted, started and glared at him with something like anger.

"It's easy for you—you haven't seen, you haven't known how salvation and damnation go into one!"

Jamie drew a deep breath. He was interested, in a repelled sort of way, and yet Mansell's maundering confession wasn't getting him anywhere. He said, "I'm sorry to be such a pragmatist, but I wish you could be a little more definite. If they've done anything against the law, why not go to the police? Was that when you left them?"

"Oh, yes," Mansell said. "I even crossed over to the Brooklyn area to live—you've read Cannon's books? You know that crossing water will put a witch off your trail? That's why I wouldn't let you come to my house; for all I knew you might be one of *them* ... come to finish my damnation."

Jamie stared at him in consternation; the big, vibrant man was shaking like a leaf. It was almost too dramatic. Jock had believed all this—

Jock was dead. Mansell—well, fear of death could explain a lot. But could a man be transformed so quickly into a trembling, fear-ridden hulk?

"And you say," Mansell said tremulously, "they have begun on you?"

"With some very concrete vandalism," Jamie said. "So I called the police. And I think I have arranged it so that the manuscript itself is beyond their reach."

"The police. You fool," said Mansell contemptuously, "do you think there will ever be anything you can prove against them?"

"I thought you might help me there," Jamie said slowly, "since you evidently know who and what they are. You can't convince me that a gang like that has never done anything illegal. You could go to the police too."

"And have your death on my conscience too?"

"You can hardly be damned more than once," Jamie said reasonably, "and if you have good intentions—"

"You can be flippant about damnation all you please," Mansell said with a sudden burst of anger. "See how you feel when you know *you* are damned!"

"I wasn't being flippant about damnation," Jamie said slowly, almost bewildered. "I thought perhaps you might help keep someone else from . . . damnation."

"Maybe." Mansell stood up. "I'll have to think about it. I couldn't give you names and addresses offhand anyhow. Look, that waiter is eyeing us; they want this table. Here, I'll pay for it."

"Oh, come, I invited you."

Mansell said slowly, "Are you afraid to accept a gift from me?"

Jamie shrugged and let him take the check. He wondered why he had thought Mansell could help him. The ex-priest was clearly unbalanced, almost, if not quite, a mental case. He followed Mansell out into the street.

It was very dark now. The square was brilliantly lit with that foggy glare of polluted light that seems, in winter dark in New York, to emphasize the thick murk overhead. Mansell hauled on his gloves and looked around with that darting of his head. "I'll have to think. I'll call you."

He turned without further good-bye and plunged into the crossing, and then, as Jamie stared after him in amazement, tires screamed and brakes squealed. Jamie leaped and grabbed his arm. For a moment, panicked, Jamie thought they would both slide under the wheels of the car; then, with another scream of tires, it was gone and Mansell was staring at him, his eyes great liquid pools of shock.

"Idiot!" Jamie said sharply. "You crossed that street as if you were dead drunk!"

Mansell said, in a slow, dazed tone, "You see. You see. I knew they were watching. Let this be a lesson to you. Get out, you fool. Get out while the getting's good. Stay clear while you can."

He shook Jamie's arm from his and dodged away, running. Jamie, startled, stood and watched him duck across the street and hail a cruising taxi. The taxi rolled away, and Jamie stood staring after him, almost unable to take it all in.

So they were after Mansell too.

Well, that at least meant his brief suspicions of Mansell were pure lunacy. Mansell had almost been killed; they had both been, near as nothing, under the wheels.

Oh, maybe the man was drunk; maybe—in fact, probably—he had been dramatizing himself. That stuff about moving across water to put them off his trail, for instance—and yet his number was in the phone book? Well, anyone who got involved with Satanists had to be a little bit nuts. But, dramatizing or no, drunk or no, he was, so far, Jamie's best clue.

I'll give him a day or so to sober up, Jamie resolved, *and then see if I can't get him to give me more information . . . if they haven't scared him right out of what little guts he has.*

Chapter Eight

THE HEADACHE WAS BACK. BARBARA, CROUCHED on her bed in a daze with the pain, kept thinking, *I must be crazy after all.*

She had not opened the door again and had pushed up a chair against it. Not that she seriously believed that either of the women would try to break in now. All afternoon, since Dana had come in uninvited and gone away again, Barbara had sat on the stripped bed not moving. But she had heard them moving around in the apartment. *My apartment and they've made me a prisoner in it!*

At least, if I don't set foot outside my own room and they throw any more foul garbage around—dead mice, crucified frogs and such stuff—they can't accuse me of doing it.

Or at least, if they do accuse me, I'll know that I didn't do it myself in a moment of insanity!

Or will I? Can I even be sure I've been here all along and not sleepwalking again? Can I ever be sure of anything again? No. If I go on like that, I will go crazy. Go crazy? I'll be crazy! Oh, if only Jamie would come home!

Her head throbbed and pulsed as if some giant had it in monstrous rhythm and was squeezing it in time to some jerky unheard music—or was it the sound of her own heart that seemed loud in her ears?

When she strained her ears to hear, she could just hear the voices of the other women in the living room. The two voices rose and fell, but she could not make out a single distinguishable word, although now and then it seemed to her that she heard her own name. Well, why shouldn't they talk about her? Oh, hell, they were probably discussing knitting patterns. One of the signs, the sure signs of craziness, is to be convinced that other people are talking about you. Poor Jerry had begun feeling that way a few months before his death . . .

No, no. Don't think about Jerry. Oh, God, why didn't Jamie come home?

The room darkened into the early darkness of December. It had begun to snow outside. Barbara smelled something cooking in the kitchen, and, even through her intractable headache and rolling nausea, it smelled good and reminded her that she had not eaten a morsel of food that day.

Were they waiting for hunger to tempt her out?

Damn. She had meant to go to the studio today. She hadn't even called her answering service to cancel her appointments, to tell them she was sick. *That's it*, she thought with instant, obscure relief. *I'm sick.* Anybody *can be sick.*

*Yes, you're sick. That's right, Barbara. You're
sick. You need rest, a good long rest. Get sick and
stay sick, so you'll be out of the way, and then no
one will hurt you . . .*

"God," she said aloud, clutching her head,
"now I'm hearing things, too!"

She tried to close her ears against the insidi-
ous whisper, but it went on and on inside her
head, relentless, toneless.

*You see how sick you are. Too sick for Jamie,
Barbara.*

You'll go crazy, just like poor Jerry . . .

"No," she said aloud again to the voice. She
stared, terrified, into the mirror over her dressing table. A white, haggard, drawn face, the face
of a woman at least forty, stared back in terror.
She thought, *I'm hearing voices, and there are no
voices. So I must be talking to myself without
really knowing it. Are they trying to convince me
I'm crazy? Or am I crazy and trying to convince
myself that someone else must be doing it to me?
It's a goddamn squirrel cage—round and round!*

In a sudden fit of fury she went into the bathroom, scrubbed her face hard with a wet washcloth, and put on makeup and a dress with
trembling hands. She was so pale that the lip
gloss and eye shadow stood out stark, making
her look like a painted clown, but the accustomed, habitual activity calmed her. She pulled
a dress from her closet, the brightest red one
she owned. But instead of looking cheerful in
the darkening room, she felt she looked garish,
defiant.

The dead mouse was gone, and the bloodstained knife, too. Probably Dana had taken them

away. Barbara hadn't seen her to do it, but that
didn't mean anything. But the charm, the little
rough-linen bag filled with obscene rubbish? That
lay on the floor behind the unmade bed. Barbara picked it up, her fingers curiously reluctant to close over it.

This was proof, she thought. But proof of what?
And proof for whom? I ought to throw it into
the fire, but I'm a coward. Didn't somebody do
that with a voodoo doll once, and go up in
flames? No, that was some stupid movie on "The
Late Late Show." Anyway, the fire's not lit and
I can't build a special fire here in the bathroom
for it!

But if I show it to Jamie? . . .

Would he accuse me of trying to get sympathy? Last night when I burned his manuscript—
well, there was another copy, so it wasn't an
irreplaceable tragedy, but if I pulled another
crazy stunt right away, he might even think *I*
was doing all this to him! Yet I don't want to
put the foul thing back in our bed. It has a—a
nasty feel to it.

The copy of *The Devil in America*, which she
had been reading earlier that day, still lay open
on her bureau, face down. A vague memory
plucked at her, and she picked it up and riffled
the pages, looking for something she half remembered.

*Folklore insists that the person finding a hex
charm or voodoo talisman, even if he is positive
that it is aimed at himself, should never destroy
it out of hand. It should be kept in safety, unable to do further harm, until it can be destroyed by some knowledgeable adept or trained*

*person who knows how to demagnetize the charm
and break the bond between it and its victim.*

Reading on, she discovered that there were
several ways of insulating a charm against further harm. It could be kept in a box of solid
silver, soldered shut with lead, and sealed. *That's
not much help,* Barbara thought. *I don't just
happen to have a silver box handy, or a soldering
iron.* Neither did she have a box of sandal or
cedar wood, to be sealed with virgin wax, preferably with a pentagram seal. *Even if I believed
such stuff, where would I get the ingredients?* It
was like trying to make up that magic potion in
Shakespeare—where in heck would anyone get
the eye of newt and toe of frog and all the other
stuff? The only possible recipe Jock had given
against such charms was that, in lieu of anything better, they should be rolled up in silk,
preferably virgin silk, whatever that was, and
kept in an airtight container. She rummaged in
her bureau drawer and came up with a pure silk
scarf she had never worn. Well, it wasn't "virgin
silk"—she assumed that meant silk that had
never been dyed or made into a garment—but it
would have to do. She rolled the nasty little bag
into the scarf, making a packet less than two
inches square, then found in her handbag a small
plastic tube she had used for a while to keep
vitamin pills in. It was probably about as airtight as anything else she could find. She thrust
in the silk-wrapped charm, forced the cap back
on, and finally sealed it with adhesive tape from
her medicine cabinet.

There. If the whole damn thing is suggestion,

I'll try some countersuggestion. But I wish Jamie would get home.

She sat down on the bed again, trying to control the shaking of her hands, but in a very few minutes she heard the apartment doorbell ringing. Jamie's special ring. Two short rings: a code signal to save him the trouble of using his key if his mother or Barbara were home.

Thank God, thank God! The endless day was over, and Jamie was here. The apartment was hers again; she was no longer trapped by hostile presences. She would go to him, wrap herself in his sanity and strength, and then show him the charm, persuade him that the danger was real.

She got up off the bed.

She did *not*. Her trembling, strengthless knees refused to obey her; strength seemed to drain out of her with every breath. She felt herself struggling as if against invisible bonds, tried to raise herself on her hands, trembled and fell back against the mattress. She lay there, her heart pounding, knowing in numb horror that now she had no defense against anything they wanted to say about her.

Jamie had to repeat his ring before the door opened; he had to conceal his irritation when Dana's fair face appeared through the crack in the door.

"Oh, Jamie," she said, in quick, low concern, "I'm glad you're here. There's trouble."

Oh, God, what now? He almost groaned aloud. "What is it this time, Dana? More phone calls?"

"Worse than that," said Dana, her sweet face troubled with a frown. "It's Barbara, Jamie. She's locked herself in her room and she won't come out. She hasn't even come out to eat all day. I went into her room to help her make her bed this morning, and she acted as if she didn't know me."

"Yes," his mother put in over her shoulder. "If Dana hadn't been here, I'd have been frightened to death—there was a bloodstained knife in the kitchen this morning. And you know how Jerry . . ."

Jamie felt his throat close in sudden fear. Barbara! Were the mysterious *they* threatening Barbara as they had done with Bess. Or had all this terrible business cracked her balance? He would have sworn Barbara was completely stable, complete free of neurosis. After Jerry's death she had consulted a psychiatrist. "If we're going to have kids, it might be a good idea to make sure it's nothing in the family," she'd said cheerfully. But the psychiatrist had pronounced her completely healthy, completely free of neurotic tendencies.

But could anyone really know?

He listened to his mother with half an ear. "I'll talk to her," he said, and went to the door of the room.

Turning the handle, he encountered pressure against the door.

"Barbara!" he called, raising his voice. "It's me. What's wrong with the door?"

Her voice sounded strange through the closed door. "Is it really you, Jamie?"

"Who in hell do you think it is—Santa Claus?" he snapped, suddenly angry. "Come on, Barb, stop playing games. Open this door like a good girl! What's gotten into you, trying to scare hell out of us all?"

There was time for him to hear his own heart thumping uncomfortably in the silence, to become conscious of Dana's face and his mother's behind him, to wonder if Barbara were unconscious or asleep or actually hiding in the bathroom, before he heard a queer sound like moving furniture. Then the handle turned and the door opened a cautious inch or two and Barbara's face, or a narrow slit of it, appeared in the narrow space.

"Come in," she said in a whisper.

"No, damn it, you come out. I'm not feeling like a lot of nonsense tonight, Barbara. I want a drink, and I want my dinner. I've had enough trouble for one day. Come *on*," he pleaded, "don't *you* start! What's the matter, Barbara, sick?"

Behind him in the silence he heard his mother whisper, "Just like her poor brother. I *told* Jamie . . ." and it made him irrationally angry at Barbara for giving his mother this kind of opening for her spite. Barbara heard it too, and her face hardened. She came into the living room, and Jamie realized that she did, indeed, look sick: she had too much makeup on or something, and her hair was disheveled, and she looked as if she had grabbed something out of the closet at a moment's notice and hauled it on. Her hands were shaking, and he saw her look quickly at Dana and his mother and turn just as quickly away. She said, "Give me a drink. Let's all have a drink. But don't expect me to eat anything they've cooked up for me!"

"Why, Barbara, darling," Mrs. Melford said,

and Jamie scowled. He went to the cupboard, then hesitated.

Dana said, "Barbara, I wouldn't drink anything if you're not feeling"—she hesitated—"all right."

"What would you care?" Barbara spat out the words, and Dana flinched. Jamie said, "Oh, come now," hardly knowing what he said. He had the usual masculine loathing of scenes, and he was realizing, slowly, that something was going on that could not be smoothed over.

Barbara went and poured herself a stiff drink from the bottle of Scotch. Her hands were shaking, and she spilled some; Jamie went and took the glass from her. He said clumsily, "Look, sweetheart—"

Barbara dropped the glass. The liquid splashed and the glass, miraculously unbroken, clattered and rolled away. She said, in a high, hysterical voice, "Jamie, I don't want her here. I don't want them here. I'm, I'm ..." She gripped her hands tightly together, struggling with herself. She said, her lips white, "I'm sorry. I know I sound like an hysterical idiot—I'm trying not to—but Jamie, Jamie *please*, can't I talk to you alone?"

"Poor Barbara," said Mrs. Melford sweetly, coming to pick up the glass. She rubbed with her lace handkerchief at the splashed liquid on the red dress. "You've made a stain on your pretty dress; it may never come out. Can't you try to pull yourself together, dear? Why don't you go and lie down, and let me make you a nice hot cup of tea, or some soup, and you just rest a little."

Barbara struck at the hand containing the handkerchief. She didn't actually touch it, but Mrs. Melford shrieked and drew her hand back. Barbara said, high and gasping, "Let me alone, don't touch me. Jamie, can't you see what they're doing? They're trying to make you think I'm crazy." She fell against him, clutching at him with her hands. "Oh, Jamie, Jamie. I'm not crazy, am I?"

He felt her trembling, rigid under his hands, and a chill of horror ran through him. He had to overcome his revulsion, a sort of sick flash of Jerry cowering in his room a week before he had shot himself, before he could put his arm around his wife, and say very gently, "Of course not, Barbara. You're sick, and I think you're a little hysterical. No one wants to hurt you."

"She *does*," Barbara said violently, "she does! No. No. I won't say it. She *wants* me to make all sorts of crazy accusations; I can feel her wanting me to. I won't do it ..." Her voice trailed off.

"Sit down," Jamie said. He pushed Barbara gently into a chair, poured her a drink. "Sip this. Sip it slowly. Now tell me, what is all this about? Dana? Mother? Did you all have a fight?"

Dana spread baffled hands, and her blue eyes were wide and innocent. "We went out shopping while she was still asleep, and when we came back she was like this."

"Mother?"

"I just don't know, Jamie. I've been worried about her for a long time. You know that."

"I didn't," Jamie said bluntly, looking at the three women with puzzled eyes. "Come on, Barbara, snap out of it. It's been a rough day for everybody."

Barbara said, "They're doing it to us the way they did to Jock and Bess. It's all in the book."

"Oh, damn the book!" Suddenly Jamie was angry. "You're imagining things. You know Mother is fond of you. Have you still got that bee in your bonnet about Mother wanting me to marry Dana?"

Barbara said slowly, as if compelled, "Will she deny it?"

Mother Melford's mouth trembled and she looked as if she were about to cry, but there was a sort of smugness behind the tears. She said, "I didn't think Barbara was the wife for you, Jamie, and now you can see how unstable she is—this hysterical nonsense. You need peace and quiet, my poor boy, no scenes and hysterics!"

"Do you see what I mean?" Barbara sounded trapped, almost frantic. "All the time hanging over me. Hating me, goading me, pushing me until I—I make scenes like this and *you* start hating me. Oh, God, Jamie, I don't want her here. I've tried, I've tried so hard, but it's no use. She hates me, and she's brought Dana here— that was the last straw—and today when I found—" She stopped short, as if something had physically sliced off her words.

"Go on," said Mrs. Melford, her voice quavering, "listen to her, Jamie. Let her stand there and talk to me like that. Aren't you going to throw me out? Aren't you going to put your own mother out in the street?"

"Mother, damn it—" Jamie clutched his hands to his head and realized suddenly that he still

had on his hat and coat, that the crisis had
erupted so suddenly he hadn't even had a chance
to take them off. He shed them and dropped
them on the end of the sofa, looking around
angrily at the women. The room felt like a hostile arena. Barbara had dropped down on the
sofa too, sobbing, and he looked down at her for
a moment with something like hatred. How dare
she do this kind of thing to him? How could she
put him into this—this hysterical soap-opera con-
frontation, complete with mother-in-law trouble and the Other Woman? For a moment it
seemed that he was looking at the three women
through the wrong end of a telescope, as if they
were small inanimate dolls on a TV screen: Barbara, shaken, disheveled and weeping; his mother
standing there pouting, the picture of injured
innocence—*almost too much innocence;* Dana
alone looking lovely, detached, her sweet face
expressing compassion and concern. He felt
drawn to her by that reflex that draws the American male toward the underdog. *Poor Dana. It's
too bad she has to be mixed up in this family row.*
Her calm seemed attractive against the background of hysteria. Against his will, he felt himself thinking, *Would she have treated me to this
kind of scene when I came home?* He smiled at
her, a little ruefully, before turning his attention
back to Barbara.

He said, "Look here—Mother, Barbara—this
is about enough of this. Do we have to air our
family differences in front of a stranger? If you've
had some kind of fight, it's sure to blow over.
These things happen in all families, I'm sure.
Mom, why don't you go out and see what's going

on in the kitchen—I smell dinner out there, we don't want it to burn—and let Barbara finish her drink in peace and all of us calm down a little. You too, Dana. Barbara wants to talk to me alone. Okay?"

They went, throwing protesting looks behind them. As the kitchen door swung shut he went and poured himself a drink and gave Barbara a fresh glass. He sat down across from her, watching her struggle to control her sobs. When at last she was quiet, he said, "Come on, Barby-doll, what's all the waterworks about? Is it Mom? Look, sweet, you know I never was crazy about having her live with us in the first place, but with the housing shortage the way it is, I couldn't afford a separate apartment for her. She hasn't a bean, not even an old-age pension. She's never worked; she was a housewife all her life. And I hate to chuck her into one of those residence hotels that are just dumping grounds for old people."

She said, struggling against sobs, "I know, Jamie. I thought it would work out."

"I thought, all things considered, that you and Mother got along all right most of the time. Was I wrong all along then?"

Barbara stared at her knees. "Until today, I didn't know how much she hated me."

"Barby, I just don't know what to say to you. You were never the kind of person to have a persecution complex."

She swallowed hard. The alcohol was beginning to flush her face a little. "You see? There isn't anything I can say, or I just have a persecution complex. It's so neat ... it all ties in so well. But this morning I found a ghastly thing in the kitchen. It was just the beginning . . ."

Jamie groaned. "Oh, my God, that damned frog? Barbie, I'm sorry. I would have sworn I chucked that thing down the incinerator shaft myself, but I was so confused with everything happening at once. But why do you blame Mother for that? It was those damn crackpots who've been trying to get me over Jock's book. Are you honestly trying to tell me you think Mother is tied in with *that* crew?"

She held her head between her hands. He irritably wished she would go and comb her hair; he had never seen her looking like this before and was enraged at himself for mentally comparing her to Dana's soignee perfection. Barbara said, "I don't know what to think." She sounded weary, defeated. "Put it that way, and you'll have me convinced that I ought to hunt up Jerry's psychiatrist again."

He swallowed the last of his drink, set the glass down, and reached for her hands. He said gently, "Did it ever occur to you, Barbara, that if this scare campaign has any point at all, the point of it is to scare us all into turning on each other? I gather they tried to do just that with Jock and Bess. If we keep our heads, we can laugh at them. They must know now that it's not working; unless they're prepared to bomb the printing press, the book's going through. Are you going to let them get to you with their stupid war of nerves?"

She didn't raise her eyes. He was, against his will, moved to sympathy. At last she said, looking up, her hands tensely knotted, "Maybe all this—the tension over the book—just brought it to a head. Maybe I never should have agreed to try living with your mother. Maybe you never should have married me against her wishes."

He tried to sound lighthearted. "I'm sorry, but that's just the way it is; I married you, and if Mother doesn't like it, that's her bad luck." He touched her knotted hand. "Maybe we can work something out, Barbie, if it's getting on your nerves. If—*when* we have children," he corrected himself, "we'd have to make other living arrangements anyhow. Perhaps we ought to start thinking about them now. But can't you put up with it until I can think of something?"

Her mouth trembled. "I'll try—for your mother. I can't make any promises, but I'll try. But when she brought Dana here—that was the lást straw. Jamie, can't you get *her* out of here?"

He was surprised at the surge of his own anger. "Barbara, that isn't worthy of you. I detest jealousy!"

"I don't care!" Her voice cracked. "While she's here, I know your mother never loses hope ... Jamie, I'm sticking to this. I'll put up with your mother for a while ... for a little while. But I want Dana out of here, and I want her out of here tonight! *Tonight!*"

"What on earth can I say to her?" Jamie demanded helplessly. "You yourself told her she was welcome to stay. How can I throw a guest out of my house ... and at this hour of the night? Where would she go?"

"I don't care what you say to her or where she goes," Barbara said, and there was a dangerous note in her voice. "A hotel. A hostel. The Salvation Army. But she's going, Jamie. Or else I am. I mean that, Jamie. Her or me. I will not sleep in my bed again with that woman under my roof!"

He stared at her. He felt utterly bewildered, as if the familiar Barbara he knew had become a stranger. He said, "I really am beginning to wonder if you've lost your mind, Barbara!"

"That's a nice, simple, easy explanation!"

"Not so very," he said. The anger was rising, against all his desire to control it. "You're not being fair or sensible, and you have no right to make that kind of ultimatum. That kind of choice—it's too melodramatic!"

She said in a low voice, "Why do you want Dana here? Why are you defending her?"

"Oh, Christ!" He started to yell, remembered Dana in the kitchen, and lowered his voice. "I don't want her here, not especially. I just don't want to throw her out!"

Her face was hardened, the Barbara-stranger again, as she said coldly, "Don't then. Throw me out instead, that's what it amounts to." She stood up, and while he watched in dismay she walked to the hall closet, took down her dark pea-jacket, and began to slip into it. She said, her voice taut and controlled, "I'm not bluffing, Jamie. If I walk out that door, I'm not coming in it again until she's packed and out of here."

He stood, angry, stubborn, his fists clenched. Something inside him was clamoring, *Let her go, go and be damned to her! By being as unreasonable as this, she's forfeited any right to your concern!* But he was horrified at its voice. He went to Barbara and grabbed her arms; she wrenched free. At his touch, she burst into racking sobs again. He put his arms around her and held her, and the mixture of anger and confusion melted a little.

He said, still simmering but making his voice gentle, "We can't go on like this, Barbara. It's ridiculous. I give in, but I'll make a deal with you. Dana goes, but tomorrow you see a psychiatrist. Is it a deal?"

He still had hopes she would indignantly refuse, give in, say what he wanted her to say, that Dana didn't matter, that she knew she was being a fool. Instead her face actually brightened a little. She said slowly, "It's a deal, Jamie."

She was hanging her coat again on its hanger, her movements slow and frozen. He turned his back on her and strode, still simmering with resentment against Barbara (she had disarmed him!), toward the kitchen.

The kitchen was steamy warm with a good smell of cooking food, laden with the familiar herbs and spices, and the teakettle whistling softly. It was incongruous to feel so unhappy and embarrassed in this peaceful place, feeling Dana's and his mother's eyes rest on him.

"How is she, Jamie?" his mother asked in a hushed voice.

"She's . . . quieter. I'm sorry, Mother—" He hesitated; how could he say it? Dana smiled, an odd smile. She said, "Jamie, I think I'd better go. Having me here is bad for Barbara . . . in her present state."

He should have felt relieved because she had saved him the embarrassment of coming out with it. Instead, paradoxically, Jamie felt another, renewed surge of anger against Barbara for putting him in this position. "I feel awful about it, Dana, but . . ."

His mother bridled indignantly. "Jamie, **Dana** is *my* guest! Barbara has no right."

"I'm sorry," he repeated, angry now at her as well as Barbara. "I know she's your friend, Mother, but my first responsibility is to my wife. Barbara is sick, she's nervous and unstrung. I have to think of her . . ." He felt as if he were nervously repeating himself. "Of course, if Dana has no place to stay . . ."

"Of course I have. I was just telling your mother—"

"And I was telling her," his mother said, "that I will not let a sick, neurotic, unstable girl dictate who can come and go in my son's home."

"Mom, please!" Dana's voice was gentle, but Jamie got the sudden impression of steel-trap strength. She turned back to Jamie with her sweet smile. "Of course your first duty is to poor Barbara, Jamie. I respect you for it. Nothing else matters now. She must be very . . . ill. I've already called a friend of mine, Jamie."

"I feel like a heel, letting her throw you out like this."

"No," she said with an enigmatic smile. "Maybe this is the best thing that could have happened." She slipped quietly out of the room, leaving him wondering what she could possibly have meant and feeling his anger at Barbara gust up again. How could she let her jealousy do this to a harmless girl, a girl who had been her friend?

He was still angry an hour later when Dana, her suitcase packed, watching out the window, said, "Oh, there's my ride," threw her coat quickly over her shoulders, and started to the door. Mrs. Melford glowered in a corner of the room. Barbara had refused to eat supper and

withdrawn into her room, where with relief
Jamie had heard her moving around, making
the bed, straightening the accumulated clutter.
Maybe, with the house halfway back to normal,
he could get some food into her. He had told his
mother, feeling vaguely disloyal to Barbara but
feeling it was the best way to keep the peace,
that Barbara had promised to see a psychiatrist,
and she had been unusually sympathetic, saying
she knew a very good man who had done won-
ders for a good friend of her own.

Now, as Dana neared the door, Jamie grasped
her hand. "Look, Dana, keep in touch."

"Of course, silly," she said. "I'll be visiting
Mom, and of course I'll want to know how poor
Barbara is, even if she has . . . turned on me.
Maybe she'll be feeling better soon and I can see
her."

Jamie picked up her suitcase. "Let me carry
this down for you."

"Oh, no, it's not heavy," but he was already
moving into the hall with it and down the stairs.
At the door she seized it firmly from him. "Now
I insist, Jamie, really, you absolutely must *not*
come out into the cold without your coat!" The
car drawn up outside the door was already
opened, and a tall form emerged in the snowy
darkness and started to speak. Dana made a
gesture and the man only seized her suitcase,
thrust it hastily inside, got back in, and slammed
the door, driving swiftly away.

Jamie, still inside the street door, stared in
puzzlement. Was he going crazy too, or was it
actually Father Walter Mansell getting out of
that taxi to usher Dana inside?

No, it couldn't be. All this was getting on his

nerves to the point where he saw strange coincidences everywhere. It couldn't be. There were—there must be—dozens or even hundreds of men in New York with that same tall, burly build, that same model of thick dark undistinguished topcoat, that same dark kind of receding hair. He had, after all, not seen the man's face: the driver had turned away too quickly.

Yet the impression persisted all the way up the stairs. He smelled supper and suddenly felt ravenous, ready to eat up everything in sight. Maybe now that she'd calmed down Barbara would be ready to eat and be civilized, even to his mother.

Late that night, struggling out of irrational, confused nightmares (he wandered through a labyrinth, with Jock Cannon trying to call him through a thick curtain; he stumbled through a corridor littered with dead toads and broken crucifixes; he wandered into a church and picked up the Bible on the altar, and it turned in his hands into a first edition of *The Devil in America;* he was being married to Barbara again, but Father Walter Mansell was the priest and his mother was giving the bride away, and when she said, "Who gives this woman to be married to this man? I do," he looked across at the bride and it was Dana, and Barbara was lying naked on the altar . . .), he woke with a sickening start and felt compelled to reach out in bed and make sure Barbara was actually there. She moaned in her sleep and turned over but did not wake, and he listened for a moment to her restless breathing and began to drift off into a half-sleep state again. At first it was the familiar procession of vague faces, hypnagogics, the images seen on the edge of sleep, and then it was voices, dimly moving in his mind, and Jamie too deep in sleep to resist or even be clearly aware of them.

It's too late for half measures. He's got to go the same way Cannon went.

Nothing must happen to him. That's the only condition I make or have ever made; nothing must happen to Jamie.

Are you in any condition to make conditions? What you want is not what we want.

She will crack soon. With her out of the way I can handle Jamie myself.

Very well. But don't wait too long.

Chapter Nine

PARK AVENUE IN THE UPPER EIGHTIES IS ELE-
gant and bears, still, something of the
nineteenth-century sophistication of city life,
before the problems of the twentieth turned city
life into urban problems. Barbara walked between the tall, gracious apartment buildings,
her coat wrapped grimly around her, looking
for the number in her handbag.

Oh, she had handled it wretchedly. It served
her right, to find herself on the way to a psychiatrist. She had let migraine, premenstrual tension, and just plain jitters stampede her into
revealing everything. She should have been calm,
sensible, matter-of-fact, charming, as Dana had
been charming. All the hold-your-man women's
books warned her that jealousy and scenes never
got anyone anywhere. She should have been
sweet and compliant, not blunt and honest. She
should have pretended cordiality even to Daná,

then taken Jamie off alone and shown him the obscene little bag she had found in their bed.

This morning she had waked with the remnants of the headache (she still had them, damn it!), and confused memory of the scene last night had made her submissive with Jamie and carefully polite even to the elder Mrs. Melford. She wished she could have found some psychiatrist other than the one Jamie's mother had recommended, but she had told herself roughly not to be paranoid. She had surreptitiously looked him up in the Manhattan phone book: he had an excellent Park Avenue address; he had the proper letters after his name; and everything seemed perfectly in order. He had even sounded, when she telephoned for an appointment, a little reluctant to see her, promising only to work her in because of a cancellation, so why should she think of him as someone eager to get his claws on her in order to tell her what a good person her mother-in-law was and demand that she immediately snap out of all this neurotic nonsense?

The building was growing old graciously, the gilt on the doors and the gingerbread carvings looking neither decrepit nor obtrusively restored. The signboard in the lobby was filled with the names of doctors, dentists, and, Barbara assumed, probably the odd psychologist. The name she had been given was on the second floor. As she climbed to it, she saw, at the head of the stairs, a woman emerging from one of the doors, a woman in the last stages of pregnancy. Barbara felt a sharp, sick pang of envy, an almost physical pain. *Right where the burn was in the picture. Oh, God, is that why I haven't been able to get pregnant?*

Inside the office from which the pregnant girl had emerged, a pleasant feminine voice said, "Leave the hall door open, Mrs. Gardner. I'm not used to this much heat, I'm afraid."

Barbara shrank against the wall as the pregnant woman, walking carefully, passed her on the stairs. On the landing three doors faced one another across the stairwell, and Barbara thought to herself, *I'm an idiot, I didn't even realize: this doctor* must *be all right; he's right here in the same building with Dr. Clinton. I must have seen his office a hundred times when I was having all those tests last year. She must have a new receptionist. Maybe I ought to make another appointment now for another checkup. But could I ever tell her I thought the reason I didn't get pregnant was because my mother-in-law was putting a hex on me? She'd probably send me right across the hall to Doctor What's-His-Face anyhow!*

She looked at the three doors, so familiar from last year. Marian Clinton, M.D.: Obstetrics and Gynecology. Dr. Paul Barnes, Dental Surgeon, by appointment only. Alexander Wynitch, Doctor of Psychology. She wondered, uncharitably, what unpronounceable and unfashionable combination of letters lurked behind the bland and unlikely *Wynitch.* Wynzcyzowski? Wynzkowwitz? Some psychiatrist, if he couldn't even adjust to his own nationality!

She glanced at her watch. The appointment was for one; it was five minutes before the hour. *Don't go in there. It's dangerous!*

She told herself firmly not to be a fool. Yet her instinct rebelled against it. Barbara had trained herself to be practical, yet behind it she had always believed firmly in intuition, and every intuition she had was screaming at her. She wanted to run.

I promised Jamie.

He'll lock you up. You'll end up worse off than Jerry.

No. It was because Jerry didn't get help that he ended up the way he did.

She looked longingly at Dr. Clinton's office. It was a friendly memory, a time of hopefulness. She wished, with a passion, that she were going there instead, pregnant.

Step in and make an appointment.

Why not? It won't take a minute.

Her head felt thick and confused again. *You're only hunting excuses.*

She turned toward Dr. Wynitch's door again. Suddenly, overcome by dizziness, she realized that she could not, *could not*, make herself walk into the psychiatrist's office.

A kindly feminine voice said behind her, "Were you looking for Dr. Clinton's office?"

Barbara turned, dizzily, to look into keen gray eyes and the face of a tall woman wearing the white uniform of a nurse-receptionist. She said thickly, "No. I wish I were; I'm an old patient of hers ..."

"Are you ill, my dear? You look a little faint."

Barbara said confusedly, "No, I'm ... being foolish. I have an appointment with Dr. Wynitch. I was putting it off. It"—she fumbled for words—"it's dreadfully hot in here."

"I was just thinking that myself," said the strange woman cheerfully. "It's why I left the door open. Would you like a glass of water? There's a cooler in the waiting room here."

"Please." Barbara stepped inside the familiar office and drank it thirstily. "Have you been with Dr. Clinton long? I don't remember seeing you."

"Oh, no," the woman said kindly, "I don't work for Dr. Clinton at all. I'm from a part-time agency; Rosemary wanted a day off to visit a sick aunt or something, so I came to fill in for the day. It's what I do. Would you like to sit down a minute? You look rather shaky on your feet. What's the matter? Something on your mind?"

"Only this appointment," Barbara said slowly, "and I wouldn't mind: I was thinking about seeing a doctor anyhow. Only I don't like to do it just because my mother-in-law bullied me into it."

The woman nodded. She had, Barbara thought, an uncommonly restful way of speaking. She was unusually tall, with fading light hair, neat enough but not fashionably arranged—it looked as if she'd washed it and brushed it and forgotten it existed—and her face, although pleasant, was not pretty. She wore a trace of lipstick and a trace of powder, and her uniform was not quite in the current fashion. Her gray eyes were bright and smiling, even though her mouth looked grave.

She said, "Well, let's face it, my dear, a woman and her mother-in-law very seldom have each other's best interests at heart unless the mother is a very unusual woman. It's a matter of two women in love with one man, pure and simple. Oh, not always—my own mother-in-law was all the mother I ever had, and I loved her very much—but nine times out of ten a woman's

mother-in-law is her worst enemy without even
realizing it. Why didn't you pick your own
doctor?"

"I don't know one," Barbara said meekly.

"So you telephone the county medical society
or your local Mental Health Association for a
recommendation," said the woman. "Or ask your
own doctor, the one you go to for headaches and
tummy upsets and when you kids have measles.
I'll tell you one thing, though, they won't send
you here; that chap across the hall isn't any
more a psychiatrist than I am; rather less." She
smiled as if at a secret. "My dear girl, don't you
even check the accreditation of your doctors?"

Barbara said, "It says Doctor of Psychology."

The woman smiled kindly. She said, "Believe
me, there isn't any such degree, or if there is,
it's a mail-order degree from some clip joint in
California, something you get by mailing in fifty
bucks. A proper psychiatrist, my dear, is re-
quired by law to be an MD—a regular medical
doctor—and to specialize in psychiatry. A psychologist—a licensed one, that is—will be listed
with the APA, the American Psychological Association. And I happen to know that the chappie
across the hall *isn't*, for I looked him up myself
for my own reasons. Look, Mrs. . . ."

"Melford," Barbara said. "Barbara Melford.
I'm a patient of Dr. Clinton."

"Well, may I make a very impertinent suggestion . . . that you see Dr. Clinton when she comes
in—she's at the hospital now, delivering a baby,
I understand—and ask her for a recommendation, if she thinks you need a psychiatrist. Or
telephone your local GP, if you prefer, or the
Mental Health Association."

"I don't think that's impertinent at all," Barbara said, feeling suddenly relieved and warmed. "I think it's a wonderful idea. I'm very grateful to you. Do you believe in intuition?"

"I certainly do," said the tall woman. "Why?"

"Because—this sounds crazy—all the time I was out on the steps there I kept feeling I really *shouldn't* go there, and now I know why. Does that make any sense? I kept telling myself I was just chicken."

"Yes, it makes sense," the other woman said. "I knew there must have been some good reason I came here today, instead of letting someone else take this day's work. So now I've justified *my* intuition. I think it's very important to check up on the qualifications of anyone you are going to ask for help. You *will* do it, won't you?"

"I certainly will," Barbara said. She hesitated, knowing she ought to go; the woman's presence was comforting, somehow, and she wanted to stay. The woman smiled at her reassuringly and Barbara somehow felt that the stranger knew exactly what she was thinking. She felt like a lost chick settled comfortably under a mother hen's wing.

The stranger said, "Oh, by the way, my name is Claire Moffatt, and—could I be very impertinent again?—before you go to a psychiatrist, have you had a physical checkup? Sometimes symptoms—especially the kind mothers-in-law notice," she added, smiling, "aren't a symptom of mental trouble at all, but some physical problem. And, let's face it, when somebody says 'You're crazy,' they may simply mean 'I don't like the way you're behaving.'"

"I had a physical checkup almost a year ago,"

Barbara said, "and until recently my only problem was that I couldn't get pregnant. My only emotional problem, that is. But lately I've been—oh—imagining things, having headaches for no reason, and last night I sort of flipped out, screamed at my husband's mother, threw a houseguest—her guest, but I guess mine, too—out of the apartment in the middle of the night, and generally acted in a way I didn't feel was *sane*. So when Jamie—my husband—suggested I see a psychiatrist, I just didn't feel able to argue."

Claire raised an eyebrow. She said, "Well, even in our overadjusted age, an outbreak of temper hardly qualifies as proof positive of needing a psychiatrist. The major law of our culture seems to be *don't rock the boat*. But even so . . ."

"Oh, I freaked out all right," Barbara said ruefully. "I was suspecting that they hated me."

"Well," Claire said, "maybe they do. Did you ever think of that? It does happen, you know. In spite of what they may have taught you in school or charm class, you can't always be popular with everybody."

"Oh, I *know* that," Barbara said quickly, "and it's true that Mother Melford wanted Jamie to marry someone else—this girl I threw out of the apartment last night. But it seems such a—such an uncivilized way to behave. And the things I was imagining were just too freaky . . . not rational." She hesitated and then, looking into the detached face of the older woman, blurted out, "I thought they were trying to put a curse on me."

Once the words had escaped her, she was sure that Claire would look at her with amazement or contempt, but the woman's face did not change. She said something very softly; it sounded like "So that was why . . ."

Barbara said, "You can see I sound like an escapee from those little men in white coats."

Claire said, "Not necessarily. Listen, Barbara. Dr. Clinton will be here in twenty minutes. She hasn't any appointments before two; suppose you see her for a few minutes. You say she knows you. If she thinks you're deranged enough to need a psychiatrist, I'm sure she can recommend one. If not, I wonder if you'd come with me to see a friend of mine? I leave here at three, and this friend of mine"—she smiled—"is something of an expert on people who go around trying to put curses on people, and all that. It does happen, you know. Last night, quite late, this friend telephoned me. He asked if I was planning to work here today, or could arrange it. I said no, I wasn't planning to, but if there was a good reason I could arrange it. He told me to come here if I possibly could because someone here was going to need help—need it very badly."

"But how would he know?"

Claire smiled. "It's his business to know things," she said. "You might call him a specialist in knowing when people need help. Someday I'll tell you how he happened to pick me up at a moment when I was going down for the third time."

It sounded as mad as anything she had imagined last night . . . as weird, as strange, as fantastic—and yet, looking into Claire's calm and kindly eyes, she realized that the woman had made no attempt to persuade or coerce her.

She resolved, suddenly, that at least it would give her a sympathetic and uninvolved ear. Sometimes it was easier to tell something fantastic to a perfect stranger.

"I'll see Dr. Clinton," she said, "and then, if she doesn't send me straight to a psychiatrist, I'll . . . go with you to see your friend." Some of her confused relief spilled over. "If he's a specialist in knowing when people need help, God knows I can use his help!"

Dr. Marian Clinton was cordial and slightly surprised. "Well, Barbara, this is a pleasure; don't tell me you're pregnant! Didn't I tell you it was just a matter of having patience?"

Barbara shook her head. "No, I'm not pregnant," she said. "Actually, I came to have you look me over—and maybe recommend a psychiatrist."

She told her story, trying to be accurate and not to spare herself. She left out the fantastic element, saying only that her nervousness had begun when some cranks had begun persecuting her husband about a book he intended to publish, that she had had an episode of sleepwalking in which she had destroyed one copy of the book, that she had become hysterically suspicious of her mother-in-law and of a houseguest; she mentioned the headaches and abnormal tension. Doctor Clinton, after asking a few routine questions, gave her a brief physical examination, then looked at her curiously. "Barbara, tell me one thing. What drugs have you been taking?"

"Drugs?" Barbara looked startled. "None. Aspirin now and then for a headache. Nothing else."

"You don't use marijuana ... pot ... grass
... anything like that?"

"No. I smoked a joint once years ago and it
only made my throat sore."

"Have you been taking any unusual kind of
headache tablets ... Cafergot, anything that your
doctor gave you, a prescription you got refilled
maybe?"

"No, I know ergot's for migraine, but I only
took it twice and it didn't really help the migraine and it made me sick, so I threw the rest of
the pills down the john. Why?"

"I don't know exactly," Dr. Clinton said, "but
you have some of the symptoms of ergot poisoning. There was a headache medicine marketed
as a miracle drug for migraine some years ago—
big splash in *Reader's Digest*, all that—a distant
relative of LSD, actually. The trouble was it
stopped some migraines, but it was viciously
addictive, it gave people high blood-pressure,
and about half the people who took it had psychotic freak-outs of one kind or another. *Sure*
you haven't been taking anything, Barbara? It's
not as if I were going to grab you for illegal
drug abuse or anything, but you should always
be honest with your doctor, your lawyer and
your priest, honey."

"What do I have to do ... say scout's honor?
Honest to God, Doctor, I'm *scared* of drugs. I
even hate to have a penicillin shot. Aspirin, Tums,
and mouthwash, that's all I ever get at the drug-
store besides Band-Aids, toothpaste, and Tampax."

"Tums? You have indigestion?"

Barbara chuckled. "I figured it was too much
coffee on an empty stomach, too much irritation

with models, too much eating on the run ...
maybe even too much mother-in-law trouble."

"It could be," Dr. Clinton mused. "Who does
your cooking?"

"Jamie's mother. Do I need a psychiatrist? I
mean, if my mother-in-law is giving me ulcers ..."

"No," Dr. Clinton said slowly, "it isn't a psychiatrist you need, Barbara. I believe you. Maybe
you need a vacation. Or"— she hesitated—"to
do your own cooking for a while. Barbara, I
want to make some tests next week. Meanwhile,
do me a favor. Eat out for a week or so, if you
can afford it. Or cook your own meals. I don't
want to get the wind up, but ... maybe you had
better think about sending your mother-in-law
to a psychiatrist. I"—she bit her lip—"I hate to
say this, but I've got to warn you. You're being
poisoned, Barbara."

Chapter Ten

ABUSY EDITORIAL OFFICE IS A GOOD PLACE TO
get away from insistent personal problems. Jamie Melford dictated nine letters
to his secretary; spent an hour with the art
editor approving designs for three new paperback Westerns, two Gothic novels, and a nonfic-
tion expose of the fashion business; talked on
the telephone with a disgruntled author whose
relatives and friends were complaining that nine
separate paperback outlets had no copies of his
latest book; chatted briefly with the head of an
authors' agency to ask for three more Gothic
novels; and finished up the morning by reading,
over a half-dozen cups of coffee, the first few
pages of a dozen novels, all except three of which
he rejected after reading half a chapter and gave
back to his secretary to return to their authors;
the others he bundled up to take home that
night and read at leisure for final decisions.
They'd probably be rejected, too—most of the

books published by Blackcock came through reputable agencies—but a conscientious editor read the unsolicited stuff too: you never knew when you'd find a minor miracle in the slush pile, sent in by some writer with more talent than marketing know-how.

This brought him to lunchtime, and while he lingered over a hot roast beef sandwich and a beer at a local chophouse, he reluctantly remembered Barbara and dutifully put in a call home in case she had news for him. But the telephone rang eight times with that odd, doleful sound of a mechanical instrument assaulting empty walls. It was like the old paradox of the tree falling in the forest, Jamie thought. Did it make any sound if there was no one to hear it? He replaced the receiver with an odd sense of relief and went back to his office.

Neither the secretary nor the switchboard girl was back from lunch, and the offices were quiet and empty, although someone had dumped a fresh load of manuscripts on his desk. He saw the gray boxes of one of the large agencies and assumed their messenger service had brought some Gothics for him to read. There were also a couple of wrapped-and-tied manuscripts; a stack of envelopes that could contain anything from fan letters to queries about books to be submitted; and the usual load of advertisements, trade publications, free samples, and the assorted junk that the Postal Service subsidizes under the mistaken impression that it is helping along the causes of literacy, education, and good business.

His secretary came in, unwrapped herself from scarves and mittens and boots, tucked a wrapped doughnut in her drawer for midafternoon, and began cutting the strings on the manuscript boxes. "Just after you went to lunch, Mr. Melford, Barry Swift called," she began. "He says Boyce called him about doing the cover for the new Cannon book—the witchcraft one. Can he come in and talk to you about it this afternoon?"

Jamie's immediate reaction was *Oh, hell.* He would have liked to spend one day at least without thinking about the confounded book. It had made enough trouble already. But time and tide—and publishers' and printers' schedules—wait for no man, and Cannon's death meant that the new book ought to be hustled into this spring list if possible. "Okay, I'll see him at two," he said, "and I'll have a couple of chapters from the Xeroxes for him to work from."

He took a couple of letters marked "Personal" that she passed to him and started to open them, while she slit the string of the manuscript boxes.

"Can we use a sexy nurse novel?" she asked.

Deep in a query letter about a suspense novel from an old reliable, Jamie grunted, "Uh uh. Nope. Nurse novels are written for fifteen-year-old girls. No sex."

"But Mitchell Hanover Associates says it's a very *good* nurse novel."

"Nope. Nurses can have a love life but no sex life, forever and ever, amen, thus spake the Lord. Tell him to send it to one of the quick-and-dirties on the West Coast."

"Okay. Mitchell Hanover ought to know better," the girl agreed. "Sometimes even the best agents send in the damnedest things—" She broke off in a short, gasping scream. "Oh, God! Ugh!"

"What's the matter, Peggy?" The girl had

scrambled up from her desk and stood back, staring in horror at an opened box that lay before her. Jamie took a quick stride toward her, then stopped, his throat closing in sick revulsion.

In the gray familiar box of one of the big agencies lay the corpse of a rat.

For a moment, unnerved, he could only stare down into the box. The girl was white and sick-looking. Jamie had to swallow once or twice before he could find his voice. "Somebody's idea of a sick practical joke, Peggy. Probably the same damn joker who tore this place up last week."

Her voice quavered. "Shall I call up the cops again?"

"Oh, hell, I don't know. I just don't know." Maybe they would feel it necessary to know that the persecution was continuing. On the other hand, what could they do about a dead rat in the mail? "This was . . . in a manuscript box?"

"Right here in a manuscript box from Mitchell Hanover."

"Well, call 'em up and ask what they hell they know about it," he insisted, and as she went on staring down at the desk where the dead rat lay, he said gently, "Go on out and use the phone at the switchboard desk, Peggy, and don't worry about it."

She went, frowning back at him, and he knew that in five minutes the story would be all over the office; *This used to be such a nice place to work.* . . . And he also knew, beyond reason, that Mitchell Hanover Associates would turn out to know nothing at all about what had come in one of their manuscript boxes.

Father Mansell's words rang in his mind: *Sup-*

*pose when you ordered dinner in a restaurant, the
waiter put a dead rat on your plate. . . .*

He stood without moving, staring down at the
stiff ugly corpse. Strange that Mansell should
have used that one particular image, his one
serious phobia, born of three endless months in
a Korean prison camp. He had not thought seriously of it in five years.

Peggy came back into the office, saying, as he
had known she would say, "Mitchell Hanover
says they don't know anything about it. I asked
how many manuscripts their messenger brought
over, and Jean—at the desk—said three. There
are four boxes here." She stared in loathing at
the rat. "If you'll get that—that *thing* off my
desk, I'll look in the other boxes and make sure
they're all what they're supposed to be."

Gingerly, as if he were picking up a live co-
bra, Jamie covered the box. He hoped Peggy did
not notice that he was trembling; in fact, he
hoped he could get to the men's room before the
queasiness he felt overcame him and he vomited. He felt a little better once the box was
covered, and he picked it up. "I'll give this to
the janitor to dispose of," he said. "I'm sorry,
Peggy."

She was slitting the tape sealing another box.
"Stay here till I'm sure what's in this one," she
demanded. "If this happens again, I'm going to
ask for combat pay!"

The other boxes contained only neatly typed
manuscript pages, and Jamie relaxed, taking the
boxed corpse out into the hall, in search of the
janitor. He gave the man the box and a folded
bill, telling him only that someone was playing
practical jokes. He had better think about some-

thing a little special for Peggy for Christmas, too: good secretaries who could actually spell weren't easy to get and were almost impossible to keep.

Was he supposed to assume that one of them, whoever they were, could interfere with, or bribe, the Mitchell Hanover messenger between his own office and Blackcock Books, or that someone could walk into his office while the switchboard girl and secretary were out to lunch and dump an unauthorized box on his desk? Maybe it would be worthwhile asking the messenger a few searching questions. Yet even if the messenger had been bribed, how could he make a federal case out of it, out of someone's having given a teenager a couple of dollars to add an extra box to one he was carrying?

Oh, well. At least it was a *dead* rat. That was sickening enough, but if it had been a live one, his secretary might be treated to the sight of her boss screaming and babbling like a lunatic. It could have been worse.

He remembered, with some chagrin, his mustering-out leave in San Francisco. He'd spent it with a girl. They'd dined at one of the world-famous restaurants on Fisherman's Wharf and gone for a walk along the docks afterward, when a squeak and a pair of red eyes in the darkness had sent him into hysterical shrieks. Of course, he'd only been four weeks out of the prison camp then, and his nerves had been completely shot. But the girl had shown nothing but bewildered contempt—"Jamie, it's only a rat!"—and hadn't gone out with him again. He'd never told anyone except his mother and Barbara about the episode. How had they known this was his

weak point? Barbara wasn't a gossip to spread
it around their intimate circle, or the publishing
business. His mother was a gossip, but she didn't
know many of his business associates and couldn't
have innocently spread it around. The other men
from the prison camp knew, but they were scattered all over the map from San Francisco to
Vietnam. Hell, was he going to buy Father
Mansell's notion that these people were psychic?

On his way up from the janitor's closet he
stopped at the newsstand in the lobby of the
building and bought a box of chocolates, which
he presented to Peggy when he came back. "Here.
Maybe these will take the bad taste out of your
mouth." She grumbled that he was going to
ruin her diet, but she did accept the chocolates,
and he knew the immediate threat of losing a
good secretary had passed over.

When the telephone rang, he tensed, then answered it himself, not wanting to subject the
girl to another of the obscene calls—by now he
was half expecting one—but it was only Barry
Swift to see him about the cover design for the
Cannon book.

Swift, in dungarees and a scruffy sailor's jacket,
looked more like a house painter than a commercial artist. He had half a dozen tentative
design layouts under his arm. He spread them
out on Jamie's desk.

"You know, of course, you'll have to get a
final okay from the art department," Jamie
warned, "but this looks good to me. Peggy, will
you get Barry one of the Xeroxes of the book?
Give him the first half-dozen chapters, and he
can look them over and see what it's about."

"You put the copies in the office safe, Mr. Melford, after the robbery."

"You had a robbery? Nothing serious missing, I hope. There's a lot of that around," Barry Swift said. "The other day a kid in my building had the lock forced on his door, and they stole two IBM typewriters and five hundred dollars worth of stereo equipment. They broke into my place, too, but all they got was a transistor radio—I've been keeping most of my stuff at my mother's place out on Staten Island. Kids, junkies, I imagine . . . did they get your typewriters?"

"No," Jamie said, "nothing except a manuscript; I imagine this was the local crackpot crew. More vandalism than robbery, really; they made a mess of the stuff on my desk." He went across the floor to the office safe, which usually contained only the copies of current contracts—it was more fireproof storage than actual safe—and, on Friday mornings, the payroll checks. He knelt and spun the simple combination lock. "Damn nonsense to keep the manuscript in here really, but this was the manuscript they got one copy of, so I made half a dozen Xeroxes—" He broke off as the door swung wide, and gasped as a black form, evil eyes glowing, leaped out at his face.

He gasped, staggering back with an inarticulate yell.

A rat! A live rate in the safe! It missed its leap for Jamie, streaked past him; he heard Peggy scream as it bulleted across the office and ran round and round, squeaking madly, looking for a way of escape. Barry Swift yelled, grabbed up a wastebasket, and chucked it at the creature; it missed, falling with a metallic clang to the floor.

The switchboard girl and young Wayne from the front office came to the door and stood there staring in amazed wrath.

"Get it! Slam the door," someone yelled. Someone else shrieked, "No! No! Chase it out!" It ran round and round; Peggy grabbed up a long ruler and ran round after it, striking out, upsetting chairs, and a pile of manuscripts on the bookcase cascaded over the floor. Jamie stood by, trembling and half paralyzed. It seemed a full half an hour, although it could not have been more than two or three minutes, before Wayne shouted, "There it goes," and the beast ran out into the hall. "It's gone—it'll hide in the walls and get out into the alley sometime."

Jamie dropped, white and shivering, into a chair. It was taking all his control not to scream. Peggy dropped into her own chair, her face contorted with disgust. "Mr. Melford, what in hell is going on here? How did that thing get in there?"

Jamie muttered, "Search me!" It occurred to him to wonder if the Xeroxed copies in the safe were still there. It didn't matter since the originals were safely locked up elsewhere, and sure enough they had not been touched. Barry Swift took the envelope, wrinkling up his face in amused disgust. "Are things always this exciting around here?"

Peggy said angrily, "I'm just about ready to quit. Damn it, Mr. Melford, this is the last straw! First dead rats and then lives ones! What next? Snakes? Mice? Bats?"

"God forbid," muttered Jamie, unnerved. He was glad Peggy's reaction was anger instead of panic, but she was looking down at him with a certain amount of contempt, or so it seemed, and he didn't blame her. He certainly had behaved like an hysterical idiot when she had done the sensible thing and chased the creature out.

"And when I go home tonight, suppose I meet the damn thing hiding in the elevator?"

"It'll find a dark place," Wayne said. "Anyhow, the exterminator is due here next week and he'll get it then."

Jamie felt that he desperately needed a drink. He lifted the overturned chair and set it on its feet. Peggy was still glaring down at him, and he said with an effort, "Peggy, I'll call the police about this, but don't get upset enough to quit. It probably won't happen again."

"That's what you said this morning," she pointed out reasonably.

"Look. Let's close the office. It's almost two. Take the rest of the day off, do some shopping, calm down. I'll see what the police can do."

She agreed at last, and Wayne said, "Forgive my mentioning it, Jamie, but you look awfully shot yourself. Why not go home yourself. The cleaning staff will deal with this mess tonight."

Jamie agreed, although he felt weak and disgusted with himself. The Christmas season was always slow in editorial offices anyhow, and there was nothing more that needed doing today. But when he was on his way home, his feet lagged. What was going to be waiting for him there?

When he put his key into the apartment door, however, everything was dark and quiet, with no lights even in the kitchen and the early winter twilight already falling. This was unusual: Barbara was not working today, and his mother usually did her shopping early in the day and by three would have been home starting dinner. Still feeling some of the demoralizing effects of panic, he went around turning on lights and made himself a stiff drink before setting down to unwrap—rather gingerly—the three unrejected novels he had brought home to read for a final decision. Damn that rat anyhow: it seemed that he could still hear the infernal squeaks at the edge of his consciousness.

Unpleasant memories spun in and out of his memory; hard as he tried to shut them out, they persisted in coming. Rocco, the nearest thing he'd had to a friend in the prison camp, his wounded hand half chewed off by the omnipresent rats one night, dying a week later of blood poisoning . . . One night when Jamie had stayed awake all one night trying to keep the damned things off his dying friend . . .

He said aloud, harshly, "No, damn it, that's all over," got up and replenished his drink. The soda had been opened and someone had left the cap loose; it tasted flat and oddly bitter. He turned resolutely back to the first of the Gothics, telling himself not to be neurotic, that if he put a record on the stereo he would be admitting he was trying to drown out the sounds of imaginary rat squeaks. Damn it, they had to be imaginary. There was an exterminator here every six weeks in this building, and garbage went straight to an incinerator. There was nothing to attract a rat.

He thought, in self-disgust, *and I had the nerve to make Barbara see a psychiatrist. Look at me!*

He sipped his drink and opened the manuscript. It seemed incredibly dull and silly, the

standard Gothic plot about a dim-witted young
girl who went as a governess to an old house,
this one in the Hebrides. He found himself wondering why anyone needed a governess anyway
in this day of baby-sitters and day-care centers
and what would prompt a girl to become one
when she could earn money as a secretary, a
stewardess, or an executive editor! The first three
chapters were routine, but possibly publishable—
although he made a mental note that a heroine
with a name like Cheryl was hardly adequate
for the Gothic atmosphere—but when the sur-
rounding Scots began talking in a bad imitation
of Robert Burns dialect intermingled with Amer-
icanisms, he bundled the thing into the box again
and began composing in his mind a savage letter of rejection: *... why on earth a young lady
with hardly the intelligence to become a governess
should think herself qualified to write novels about
them ...*

Damn it, what *was* that noise if it wasn't rats
squeaking? Jamie got up uneasily and looked
into his and Barbara's bedroom, which lay
empty, the beds unmade. Evidently the household was more demoralized than he realized.
Bathroom and kitchen showed no sign of rodent
intruders. *Naturally not. You've got rats on the
brain, and now you think you're hearing them.*
Damn it, Barbara ought to be home now.

Mentally he jeered at himself. *So you're afraid
to stay alone in a nice, dry, clean apartment because your hear imaginary rats ...*

But could these people with their campaign of
terror—whoever they were—actually make him
believe he heard rats? The ones in the office had

been real enough, God knows, one dead and one alive.

He sat down again, picking up the second manuscript. It was a straightforward "puzzle" detective story, imitation Chandler perhaps, but after all, Chandler was dead and wasn't complaining, and it was still a popular genre. Since damned few commercial writers could be original, it was better for them to imitate good writers than bad ones! And some very good pulp writers—Leigh Brackett, John D. MacDonald—had admittedly started out imitating Chandler, after which they developed styles so good and definite that now newer writers were often accused of imitating *them*!

It held his interest through the fourth chapter, although he penciled a brief note or two about missing or obscure clues in the margin. Then he began to hear the squeaks again.

No. This time he wasn't imagining it. If there was such an animal as a rat on the face of the earth, these were the squeaks of rats. He could hear their squeaks, the scrabbling of their feet, their rustling and gnawing sounds in the darkness beyond the hall. . . .

Jamie Melford swore harshly and got up, dropping the manuscript on his chair. Damn it, he would settle this once and for all. The squeaks and the rustles made him feel sick and faint. He went into the kitchen and listened, turning on every light in the room, the fluorescents over the sink, the special range light. No signs of any four-footed creature, cat, rat, or dog. Of course not—how would they get in here? Telling himself he was being foolish, he opened every door of every cupboard in turn, seeing only orderly rows of canned soups, little jars of herbs, jars of fruit or jelly. *That rustling.* He flung open the bread box, bracing himself for a gray and evil shape to leap out at him.

Nothing. Of course there was nothing there.

But the squeaks went on.

He repeated the search in bathroom, broom closet, and linen closet, his tension rising, biting his lip as he opened each of the dark doors. Nothing, but the squeaks, the rustles, the curiously purposeful sounds went on and on. He could not convince himself now that they were his imagination, but how in God's name—*not that God would have had anything to do with it!*—could such a number of rats have gotten into an apartment this size? *The place must be swarming with them!*

His heart was pounding madly. He went back into his bedroom, flinging open closets and bureau drawers without result, and the squeaks rose to a crescendo that half drowned out his footsteps. By now he was whimpering, moaning softly to himself, ready to curl himself up in a ball, but he forced himself to go into the bathroom. From the sounds he would have sworn that the creatures were actually running over his feet, as if he stepped through a sea of swarming filth, yet in the bathroom the green and white tiles were clean and smooth, with nothing out of place but Barbara's green mermaid-patterned shower cap lying on the edge of the tub.

He laid his hand on his mother's bedroom door. They had to be in there. There was nowhere else they could be. He'd searched the apartment everywhere else. . . .

The door was locked. He stood with his hand on the knob, moaning softly aloud, fighting desperately against panic. The rat-squeaking, rat-rustling, rat-gnawing sounds went on and on, and he felt an uncontrollable drawing back, a spasm in his calves, a clutch at his heart, a shrinking of his genitals. Abruptly he dashed into the bathroom and vomited, leaning over the toilet and retching uncontrollably, the tearing spasms going on and on until he was heaving great, dry, sick sobs, his stomach empty, but still unable to control his sickness.

He wet a washcloth in icy water and washed his face, struggling for a shred of sanity.

There are no rats here.

Damn it, I hear them!

Quiet down, you're imagining things. That business at the office has you all unnerved.

Yeah, big brave Jim Melford, standing here and heaving your guts out because you think you hear a rat! This stuff can't hurt you. . . .

Oh no? Jock Cannon is dead, damn it, dead . . . dead and buried because these people got after him. . . .

But I don't believe in it. Suggestion can't kill you unless you believe in it.

But wait a minute, damn it, they've already got me hearing imaginary—or at least invisible—rats! Evidently the fact that I don't consciously believe a word of this stuff isn't enough. They can still play hell with my mind. . . .

He stepped out into the hall again. More and more it sounded as if the noises were coming from behind his mother's locked door. *They must be swarming all over the floor. Maybe she is in*

*there, maybe they've eaten her alive . . . damn it,
you must be losing your mind . . .*

"Mother!" he called aloud.

No sound except the rat squeaks, louder and
louder. Jamie rattled the locked door; then, struggling against sick nausea, flung himself against
the door, bruising his shoulder. Again and again
he threw himself against the door, while the
shrieking of the rats drowned out the pounding
of the blood in his ears.

The locked door burst open.

And at that moment every light in the apartment went out.

In the darkness the rustling, squeaking, gnawing noises rose to a crescendo. They were all
around him. They were running over his feet,
they would run up his legs, they would eat him
alive. . . .

Standing in the darkened apartment, Jamie
Melford began to cry. . . .

The doorbell rang.

It rang again, and a third time, before Jamie
mustered enough strength to grope his way
blindly toward the hall door. Barbara? He called
out, "Who's there?" through the thick miasma
of rat sounds that threatened to drown out every scrap of his consciousness.

There was no answer. Bracing himself for some
other obscene assault on his consciousness, Jamie
jerked the door open.

Dana Becker stood there, her sweet face startled by the suddenness of the opening door. She
looked clean, trim, well-groomed. She was wearing a short white fur coat and below it a skirt of
violet-and-blue plaid. Her fair hair was wind-

blown. He blinked, unable to shift mental gears
so rapidly.

"Dana?"

"Why, yes. It seems I left my social security
card in the top drawer of your mother's bureau,
and I need it for a job interview. Do you mind if
I got in and get it?"

"Mother's not here," Jamie said. It was all he
could do to organize his thoughts that far. *Now
she'll hear all this and know I'm not imagining . . .*

"I know where it is, and your mother won't
mind," Dana said. "She told me to come here
and get it. Jamie, what's the *matter* with you?
Are you sick?" She looked from the lighted hallway into the dark room behind him. "Why were
you sitting in here with all the lights out?"

"I wasn't. They just went out. Don't you
hear? . . ." It seemed strange to him that his
voice could be heard over the noises of the rats,
but Dana stepped inside, tilting her head to
listen.

"Hear what?" she asked at last.

"The rats . . . the rats . . ."

"I don't hear anything," she said, and Jamie
heard himself moan aloud. *I am insane, then.
Rats that only I can hear . . .*

"Let's get some light in here," she said, and
went past him, moving as unerringly as a cat in
the dark out into the kitchen and the pantry
behind it. She opened something. "I'll bet there's
a blown fuse somewhere, that's all. Do you have
a flashlight? I know Mom keeps one here somewhere. Ah, yes. And there are spare fuses right
in the box . . . fine." She twiddled something.
The lights flickered on.

"Poor Jamie, you look completely demoralized," she said gently. "Let me get my card from your mother's room before I forget, and then I'll come back and you can give me a drink and tell me all about it."

She vanished through the hallway; he heard the door close behind her. He wondered, as he stood in the kitchen where the rat noises were faint, what she would make of the burst lock on the door. He came slowly back toward the living room. It was worse than he had thought. There were no rat noises; there never had been any. . . .

They were gone. There was dead silence in the living room except for Dana's light steps, returning.

Could he only hear them when he was alone, then?

Would they disappear as soon as anyone else appeared?

"Now, how about that drink?" Dana said. She had thrown aside her coat. "Or is Barbara going to throw another hysterical scene if I stay?"

"Barbara isn't home," Jamie said. He felt vaguely guilty. "Anyway, she's seeing a doctor. She's going to be all right."

"Well, then." Dana settled down on the end of the sofa, crossing her long slim legs. "How about that drink? No, no soda for me, thanks."

"I wasn't going to give you any. I think there's something wrong with it . . . it tastes funny," Jamie said. "Ice?"

"No thanks, don't bother going out in the kitchen for it. Aren't you going to join me, Jamie? You look as if you could use something."

Jamie poured her drink and added one for himself. He said, "Just one hell of a day; our office practical joker has been playing on my nerves." He told her, briefly, about the rats.

"You look as if you could use a good stiff tranquilizer," Dana said. "Does Barbara have any around?"

"You know Barbara," he said wryly. "She's the original antidrug girl, won't even take cold medicines. There are times, like this, when I think maybe she overdoes it."

Dana rummaged in her handbag for a tiny gold pillbox. "Take one of mine then. It can't possibly hurt you, and it will calm you down before anyone else comes home and finds you all unstrung."

Jamie had been worrying about that a little. Nevertheless, he looked askance at the small white pill Dana handed him. "Is it okay to take it on top of whiskey?"

"Oh, sure, that's just folklore," Dana said very offhand. "If anything, the whiskey will help it work faster."

Jamie swallowed the small tablet. He felt weak and exhausted, and the whiskey, on his empty stomach, made him feel fuzzy and unfocused. He leaned back on the sofa, half closing his eyes. After the emotional exhaustion of the last hour, he felt wrung out.

It was very quiet in the room. Dana seemed very quiet, sipping her drink, her long bare legs stretched out in front of her, but motionless though she was, there seemed an almost electrical activity, as if the air around her was vibrating. A curious peace descended on Jamie. He thought it might be pleasant to light a fire, that perhaps he should telephone Barbara at her studio in case she had gone there, that he ought to be wondering where his mother had gone, but it seemed that all these thoughts came to his mind in order that he should have the pleasure of refusing to do all these things and enjoying the quiet and inactivity.

Through the quiet he became aware of an odd, monotonous little tune, a soft hum like a bee on a summer day. Dana had put her drink aside and now bent over her lap, her hands moving on something. He watched, incurious, not moving. He thought for a moment that she was knitting or crocheting, but there were no hooks and needles, no work in her lap, only her slim fingers moving smoothly on looped string and knots.

There was a strange fascination in the moving loops, as if he could not look away if he wished ... not that he wanted to look away. At last he said, hearing his own voice dull and drowsy, "What are you doing?"

"Tying knots." Her voice was very soft.

"What for?"

Now her voice seemed to come from very far away. "To catch your soul, of course. Didn't you know I've always wanted it?"

He chuckled, a soft, sleepy, silly sound. What nonsense! That Dana, what a girl! "What, a sort of lady Mephistopheles? I don't imagine my soul would bring ten bucks on the open market," he murmured through the delicious lassitude that was stealing over him. "And what are you going to do with it when you catch it?"

She smiled and drew the last knot tight. "Why, feed it on honeydew and the milk of paradise, of course," she murmured, rising purposefully from her chair. She bent over him, her slender hands

caressing, kneading the back of his neck. The
soothing little croon went on and on.

"So long as you don't feed it to the rats," he
murmured. He was falling asleep where he sat,
he realized, and knew he should get up, but the
soothing, sensuous massage of the soft fingers
on his neck robbed him of all will. Simultaneously random images spun through his mind,
the image of rising up and tearing the clothes
off Dana where she stood, or of sinking down
deeper and deeper into this dreamlike sexy
warmth and sleep.

"Oh, no," she murmured. "I've got better things
to do with it. . . ."

But Jamie Melford did not hear.

Chapter Eleven

ALL ALONG FIFTH AVENUE THE SHOP WINDOWS were crammed with holly, wreaths, decorated trees; from every store front the sound of carols pealed out. Barbara walked blindly, not seeing the gaiety of the decorations. From inside Lord & Taylor a woman's choir—recorded and amplified—in strange contrast to the merry sounds of "Jingle Bells" and "Joy to the World," sang plaintively and softly the old Coventry lament.

> O sisters two, what shall we do
> For to preserve this day
> This poor youngling, for whom we sing
> Bye, bye, lully, lullay.

Barbara felt tears stinging her eyes and bit her lip hard against the settling down of uncontrollable panic. She had walked, in blind

terror and disbelief, for the last hour, struggling
with her own emotions.

It's not my imagination then.

The word *poisoned* still rang with all its hideous strength in her memory. Not that she'd
accepted it all at once, but there it was.

All the symptoms of ergot poisoning.

Dr. Clinton had said, "That could explain why
you haven't gotten pregnant, too. It could explain a lot of things. It wouldn't be enough to
kill you, just enough to undermine your health
gradually, disturb your mind."

She had always known that Jamie's mother
had no love for her. Quite truthfully, she had
always disliked the older woman, although she
had done her best to conceal—no, genuinely to
overcome—her dislike. But how could she possibly tell Jamie about this? He wasn't a mother's
boy; in fact, there were times when she had
thought he had little more love for his mother
than she had. He had been the child of divorce
and after his fifteenth year had chosen to live
with his father, despite his mother's struggles to
keep him. Only when his mother had become
old and impoverished had he agreed to give her
room in the house, and that was mostly out of
duty. But love or no, you just *couldn't* tell your
husband that his mother was trying to poison
you, had probably been poisoning you slowly
for nine or ten months!

A nearby church carillon struck three, then
began an unfamiliar carol whose words slowly
took shape in Barbara's mind.

O come, o come Emmanuel
And ransom captive Israel

That mourn in lowly exile here
Until the son of God appear.

How sad so many of the old carols were! Barbara wished, suddenly and passionately, that she were a believer, that she could go into one of the local churches and lay her troubles on God; it seemed that there was no kind of human help available. But judging by the sadness of so many of the Christmas songs, perhaps worshipers of God, too, struggled through darkness and misery, with no help except an intangible promise, a light showing somewhere. ... Bess Cannon was a devout Catholic, yet Jock had died, snatched away by evil forces. Barbara accepted, dimly, that somewhere in the last three or four dreadful days she had begun to believe in Jock's death as the result of deliberate, malignant evil. Was there any help anywhere?"

"Hullo," said Claire Moffatt's cheerful voice, right at her elbow. "I thought maybe you'd forgotten, but it's three o'clock, and just as I promised, here I am. Let's take a taxi. You look completely worn out."

Barbara asked, as Claire raised her arm and a yellow cab slid to a halt (was it magic that found a taxi in the Christmas rush on Fifth Avenue?), "Where are we going?"

"As I said, to see a friend of mine. He's good at helping people with problems that look completely insoluble in human terms."

"That's just what I need," Barbara said bitterly. Her voice caught and she choked back a sob, resolving fiercely that she would not cry ... she simply was not going to cry. ... With sharp suspicion she demanded, "He's not a priest or some kind of religious character, is he?"

Claire laughed. Her laughter was like her eyes, bright and merry, but with an underlying calm. She said, "Not in the sense you probably use the word, although, if you define religion as trying to do what needs doing when it needs to be done, I suppose you could call Colin religious. But I give you my word he won't try to save your immortal soul or—what's that catchphrase the Jesus freaks use?—make you 'accept somebody as your personal savior.' You ought to hear him on *that* subject—insolence is the least of what he calls it! No, Mrs. Melford—hey, may I call you Barbara? There's something silly about two grown women carefully Mrs.-ing each other. No, Barbara, my friend isn't a shill for the church, and neither am I." She smiled with such sudden kindness that Barbara thought she would cry again, and said, "Was your appointment with the doctor pretty rough? You came out looking as if you'd been pole-axed. Did she give you some bad news?"

Barbara found her voice. "Just about the worst," she said. "It seems ... it seems—oh, God, I still can't believe it—it seems somebody's trying to poison me."

Claire drew in a quick breath. She said, "Okay, kid, take it easy. Wait till we get where we're going, and tell Colin all about it."

She was silent while the cab crawled through downtown traffic, turned into a side street in the west twenties, and finally drew up before an old brownstone house. Claire paid the driver, tipped him modestly, and drew Barbara along toward the steps. She touched the bell of the

first-floor apartment in a single short ring,
paused, rang twice again. After a minute a buzzer
sounded and Claire drew Barbara through the
unlocked door and turned right to an old, arched
apartment-door that had once, perhaps, been
the elaborate door of some Victorian household's
front parlor. She rapped softly. A bolt drew back,
and a man stood in the doorway.

"Hello, Colin," Claire said. "You were right,
as usual. Let us come in; this poor child could
use some tea and some sensible advice. I haven't
heard the whole story yet myself. Barbara, this
is Colin MacLaren."

Barbara's first impression of MacLaren was
only one of height, age, a look of strength—and
of the eyes. She thought, inarticulately, that his
eyes were like Claire's, calm and pleasant, pools
of peace behind whatever surface impression of
passing moods he might display. He ushered
them in and said, quite as if it were the ordinary thing for perfect strangers to turn up red-
eyed and half hysterical on his doorstep, "Come
along in. Put your coat over there. As usual, this
place is an unholy mess. You'll have to ignore it.
Claire, can I be a male chauvinist pig and ask
you to make some tea? I don't care *what* the
feminists say, it always tastes better when a
woman makes it."

Claire laughed and crossed the big, untidy
room, which was crammed with books and papers lying in heaps, to a half-door at the back.
She said, "It has nothing to do with feminism,
Colin; you could make tea as well as I do if
you'd wait until the water was really boiling
and heat the pot first. And it helps to use bot-
tled water instead of what the city of New York

laughingly calls water. You're always telling *me* not to be impatient for results!"

As she vanished into the kitchen he called, "Somebody left me a Christmas fruitcake; you might try cutting a piece or two, if you can find a clean knife and plate," and turned back to Barbara with a smile.

"Here, let me find you somewhere to sit. He scooped half a dozen books off a chair and laid them, still carefully piled, in a corner. "Good heavens, what cluttered lives we lead these days! I seem to be swimming in what Holmes called 'a thin solution of books'—Oliver Wendell, not Sherlock."

"Books don't bother me," Barbara said, smiling at his infectious smile. "My husband is an editor, and I'm used to manuscripts all over the house." She took the offered chair, sinking back in relief, realizing that she was frozen to the bone. It seemed she had spent most of the day walking up and down the street, first in apprehension, later in stunned acceptance of panic. Colin's apartment was clean enough, the one enormous room littered with books, papers, and a much-battered typewriter on a card table, but no furniture except two or three armchairs; a bed with a much-washed and faded Indian paisley spread drawn over it to make it look like a studio couch, in an alcove at the far end; and, behind a door, the kitchen from which Barbara now heard the sound of a whistling teakettle.

"The panacea of the English," Colin MacLaren said. "I hope you don't dislike tea. In this day when the coffee break seems to be an American institution, I'm treated as if I'm vaguely un-American and as if my next move would be to

overthrow Mom's apple pie by force and violence every time I go into a restaurant. They say,
'You mean you don't want any *coffee?*' It's worst
at breakfast; most places just pour it without
asking."

"No, I like tea," Barbara said. Claire came
through the kitchen door carrying an enormous
old wooden tray with a china teapot, a plate of
sliced cake, and several cups. She poured for
them. "Cream or lemon, Barbara?"

"Oh. Neither, thanks. Just a little sugar."

"My parents were Anglophiles," MacLaren said,
liberally sugaring his tea and adding a dollop of
milk. "I was brought up on this stuff, and there's
something to be said for 'the cup that cheers but
does not inebriate.' Not that I have any objec-
tions to a good stiff belt of whiskey now and
then, but I think you lose half the fun of cock-
tails by making them as ritual as bread and
butter. Have a piece of cake, Barbara—do you
have another name?"

"Melford," she said, and Colin MacLaren almost dropped the plate of fruitcake.

"So that's it," he muttered. "No—excuse me,
Claire, something else—are you by some chance
any relation to Jamie Melford, at Blackcock
Books?"

"My husband," Barbara said, "you know him?"

"I've met him quite recently. Hmm ..." He
took a piece of fruitcake and bit into it. "Drink
your tea, Barbara, you look cold."

"It's surprising how comforting tea and cake
can be in midafternoon," Claire said. "From my
own training, I know it's probably just the effects of raising the blood sugar at a low spot
between lunch and supper, plus the psychologi-

cal effect of a pleasant change of occupation, but there seems something almost magical about it."

"Who's to define what's magical and what isn't?" MacLaren shrugged. "Well, Claire, how about a report on Mission Whatsit? I take it Barbara here is the one? What's wrong?"

"She says it's mother-in-law trouble," Claire said. "I think it's more than that. I made her see her own doctor for a physical checkup, so we could rule out the possibility of a deranged mind. So—Barbara, why not tell Colin the whole story . . . what you told me, and the rest?"

Barbara set down the remnants of her fruitcake. She looked around the quiet room, grabbing for courage and calm. She said, "Maybe you'd better not rule out a deranged mind, Claire. Dr. Clinton said I didn't need a psychiatrist, but . . . I'm wondering if I do, after all, because what she said sounds so lunatic, even to me. She thinks I'm being poisoned—with ergot—and that could disturb my mind. So maybe all that hysterical stuff I told you *is* just a persecution complex, after all, because I just can't imagine Jamie's mother doing that kind of thing. That would mean *she'd* have to be crazy. And if I'm being poisoned—I mean, I read once about a woman who was being poisoned by arsenic and it was the wallpaper in her apartment that was colored with Paris green or something. And there are those kids who get lead poisoning from cheap paint. . . ." Her voice trailed off.

"Wait a minute." Colin's voice was deep and slow. "Remember, Barbara, I don't know what you told Claire. Try to start over, and tell me the whole thing."

Barbara repeated what she had told Dr. Clinton, her hysterical accusations of Dana and her mother-in-law, her sleepwalking. "Jamie tells me I burned one of his manuscripts. It was all right, he had another copy on the sideboard, but I never did a thing like that before. . . ."

MacLaren's eyes narrowed, sharp and sudden. "Wait a minute," he said. "Of course! Jamie Melford! That's how it all fits together. I was sure there had to be some connection to that crowd. Barbara, what *was* the manuscript you tried to burn? Do you mind telling me?"

"No, of course not," she said.

"Better yet, Barbara, let me tell you. Was it by any chance John Cannon's new book on witchcraft—a sort of expose of some local people?"

Her eyes widened in terror. "But if you knew that," she whispered, "you've got to be one of them, one of the people who have been trying to scare Jamie into——"

"No." His hand reached out and gripped her wrist, and after a moment her fear drained away. He said firmly, "No, Barbara. On my word of honor, I have nothing to do with them. It's true I did visit your husband the other day to suggest that he either withdraw the book or censor it slightly, but my methods are limited to explaining my reasons for wanting him to do it and relying on his own better judgment. I was afraid they were continuing with their intimidation, and I was a little fearful that he might come to some physical harm. But I had no idea, when I sent Claire out to work for Dr. Clinton today, that it had any connection to this, and even now it seems farfetched. You say you've been poisoned?"

"But how could that have any connection——"

"I don't know," MacLaren said, troubled. "You say there's been trouble with your mother-in-law for months?"

"Years."

"And what we have to call *l'affaire Cannon* only came up within the last month or two," MacLaren said. "Yet it seems entirely too far-fetched that there could be two separate plots both centering upon you and your husband. There's got to be some link somehow." He bit his lip and seemed to sink deep in thought. Finally he said, "Barbara, did your mother-in-law know Jock Cannon?"

"As far as I know, she never met him."

"And you say the trouble with her isn't recent."

"Oh, no. It began when Jamie married me. She wanted him to marry a friend of hers." Barbara bit her lip, her face working. Then she said, "One thing *isn't* imagination. I found this in our mattress yesterday."

She dug in her purse and fished out the sealed bottle. As she unwrapped the silk, MacLaren said sharply, "I thought you didn't know anything about such things. Where did you learn to do that?"

Barbara said meekly, "It was in one of Jock's books."

"Yes, I see." He took the bottle in his hand, stripped off the tape, opened it; his face contracted in disgust as he tipped out the contents of the little bag. "Ergot, the testicles of a rabbit, a lock of your own hair and your husband's, and your photograph mutilated. Ugh!" He shook it off his hand and went out through the half-door. Barbara heard him washing his hands. He came back looking sick. "A particularly nasty kind of voodoo or hex magic."

Claire said, "Barbara, forgive me for asking this, but can you absolutely be certain your husband . . ."

Barbara said quickly, "I'm positive!"

MacLaren said, "Is that wifely loyalty and feminine intuition, or reasonable knowledge?"

She shot back swiftly, "He didn't have to marry me. There were four or five women who wanted him, and Dana—the girl his mother picked—was a lot prettier. And if he was hexing me, he'd hex me to *get* pregnant, not to keep me from it!"

"That sounds circumstantial enough," Claire agreed. Colin MacLaren went into the kitchen again and fetched an asbestos pad—the kind used under pots to keep stews from burning—and a box of kitchen matches. He said, "We'll get rid of this foul thing immediately, at least. It seems as if John Cannon's would-be expose of witchcraft may have trod on some toes in your own household, Barbara, but I can't accuse anyone sight unseen. What sort of woman is your mother-in-law? No"—he stopped her when she would have spoken—"that isn't a fair question. But would you trust me to come to your house, just to get a—well, a look at her? I tend to exonerate your husband—I saw him the other day, and I didn't get the impression that he was the kind of man who'd be capable of this—but I can't help until I'm sure."

Barbara said in surprise, "Then you *believe* in all this stuff? It's not just suggestion, psychotics with overactive imaginations?"

Claire said quietly. "It's suggestion—and other things. Maybe it's suggestion carried to such a fine art that it's as tangible as radio waves or electricity—you can't see or measure those, either. I'm a psychologist, Barbara. At least, that's where I began. Then I began to realize that there were forces in the human mind that couldn't be explained in terms of the id, the libido, and the Oedipal situation, and then I began working with Colin here."

MacLaren said quietly, "You've had a sample of what these people can do, Barbara. I don't want to frighten you, but I remind you that Jock Cannon *is* dead. I have no stake in this, except I've spent my life trying to track down and smoke out this kind of thing. It's strange how it all fits together," he added meditatively. "I must be doing *something* right. Last night I was stymied; your husband wouldn't listen to me and the law I live under forbids me to interfere, so I accepted that I was blocked on that for now. Then I got a definite indication that, in the building where Claire works sometimes, someone was going to need help. I didn't know whether it was someone looking for an abortion, or someone going to that fake psychiatrist there, or just someone needing to be cheered up after learning that she was going to lose all her teeth and have to wear dentures—for a woman under thirty, Claire tells me, that's a matter for psychological counseling! But I just had an indication someone there needed help, and I sent Claire, and now ..." He got up, reaching for his coat. "I think I'd better see who lives in your household, Barbara."

"Jamie," she gasped. "Could they be doing anything to Jamie? Oh, please, can I use your telephone?"

"Be my guest. Right in there by the bed."

Barbara crossed the room, oblivious to Claire and Colin behind her, and dialed the familiar number in a frenzy. It rang twice, and then the receiver was lifted with a click. But there was no familiar "Hello," only a curious waiting, an empty, hollow sound, and then someone breathing.

"Jamie?" Barbara said, tentatively. "Jamie, it's Barbara."

She had just begun to wonder if she had a wrong number, when, at the other end of the line, there was a diabolical peal of laughter. She clung to the telephone, feeling her heart stab with pain, unconscious of Claire moving swiftly to hold her up.

The fiendish laughter went on and on. Then, abruptly, someone hung up the receiver and Barbara stood holding the handset, listening to the dial tone in horror.

"Jamie," she said, shakily, "someone was there with Jamie, laughing. I must get home! Oh, God, what's happening in my apartment!"

Chapter Twelve

I T WAS CLAIRE WHO FINALLY TOOK THE EMPTY BUZZ-
ing phone from Barbara's hands and replaced
it. Barbara twitched as if galvanized. "I must
go, I've got to get home right away."

It was a moment before she heard Colin
MacLaren, patiently repeating. "What happened?
Did you hear it, Claire?"

Barbara said, "Nothing—I mean, whoever it
was didn't *say* anything, just horrible laughter.
Oh, God, what are they doing to Jamie?" She
ran back into the main room and snatched up
her coat.

"Easy," MacLaren said firmly. "You don't even
know that your husband is there, Barbara. This
could be just another skirmish in their war of
nerves, and what they want is for you to do just
what you're doing—to rush off half cocked, never
to stop and *think*, to keep you so much off balance that you won't even look for help."

"How do you know so much about what they're

176

doing? Unless you're one of them ... oh, God, I'm sorry," Barbara said helplessly. "I know it sounds paranoid, but after today how can I trust anyone? ..."

Mac Laren said quietly, "It's reasonable caution; after what you've been through the last few days, you're probably right to suspect and test everyone. But ask yourself what stake I could have in keeping you away from your husband at this point or what I'm trying to get you to do."

Barnara said, "Nothing, so far. ..."

"Precisely. If you'll wait for about five minutes, Claire and I will go round there with you and see what's to be done. As for how I know what these people are trying to do, all I can say is that I've spent my life, or a good hefty chunk of it, trying to keep people like this from misusing this kind of knowledge."

As he spoke, he was deliberately pulling an ancient topcoat out of a closet. Claire, picking up her coat, said, "Shall I phone for a taxi, Colin?"

"No, I'll call the garage and have them bring down my car," Colin said. "This might lead us anywhere from the Bronx to Queens or even right out of the city. In any case, we might need the tool kit, Claire, so get the things out of the cupboard. You know what we'll need as well as I do."

"Right." Claire went to a long cabinet against the west wall. Barbara got only a glance inside but noted that quite unlike the rest of the apartment it was immaculately clean, with strange items neatly stacked in rows. Claire took a small suitcase from the lowest shelf, snapped it open, and said, "I have a fair idea of what we want, but is there any scrying to be done?"

"Might be. Bring along the materials, unless you want to improvise on the spot," Colin said, dialing a number. "Hullo, Cornby Garage? MacLaren here. Will you bring down my car so I can pick it up right away? When? Half an hour ago? Damn it!" He hung up, took the suitcase from Claire, and motioned them both to pull their coats tight and precede him. "The garage is right around the corner. Let's go."

Once he had swung into action he moved swiftly; the women could hardly keep up with him as he hurried down the steps, out into the street, along the block, and round the corner. The garage door gaped open and an elderly green panel truck was already at the exit, the engine running, the exhaust white against the darkening street. "Get in, girls." He slammed the door behind them. "Address, Barbara? I only know your husband's office address."

Barbara was used to the wild driving of the average New York taxi driver, and at first it seemed that MacLaren drove with great deliberation, almost always yielding the way in traffic, but after a few seconds she revised her opinion: he drove with courtesy and never pressed for an advantage or jumped a light, but he did not lose a second anywhere, darting in and out of openings in the traffic, which, had he gone only for speed, he might not even have seen. In about half the expected time he drew up in front of their building.

"You'll get a ticket if you park here," Barbara warned him.

"Maybe I will and maybe I won't," MacLaren said serenely. "At this particular moment, looking for a parking place would cost me more than a ticket, so if I get one I'll pay it. But I have a special license from the police. I almost never take advantage of it, so maybe now when I need it I'll be lucky." He seemed to move unhurriedly, but he was out of the car and up the steps even before Barbara could catch up with him and get out her key.

Barbara's heart caught with apprehension as she put her key into the lock . . . the diabolical laughter still seemed to ring in her ears. But the living room was empty. Two cocktail glasses still stood on the coffee table, and Jamie's briefcase gaped open, a manuscript set down opened at page 191. Barbara, apprehensive with the letdown, called out shakily, "Jamie? Jamie, are you home?"

Silence. Claire and MacLaren, stepping into the room behind her, exchanged eyebrow-lifted glances.

"He *was* here," Barbara said, bending over to touch the briefcase. "He had this with him this morning, and it's before his regular time to get home. . . ."

"It looks as if he'd left in a hurry," MacLaren said and picked up one glass and sniffed at it. "Nothing in here but whiskey. The other glass—any way of telling who might have been here, Barbara?"

She shook her head. "Jamie's mother doesn't drink, but it could have been anyone, somebody from the office . . . except that nobody from the office has that kind of laugh—" Her voice cracked again.

Claire's hand, hard and steady, closed on her wrist. She said, in a low voice, "Steady. Don't borrow trouble."

MacLaren was standing very still. He said, "I don't get the impression that there's anyone alive in the apartment. Just the three of us. But let's check the other rooms, just to be sure." As they went into the empty kitchen, he frowned faintly and said, almost to himself. "Not a good atmosphere here. It isn't likely this could have built up in the three days or so since Cannon was killed. What do you get, Claire?"

"Something uncommonly nasty," said Claire, frowning a little, "but not violence, exactly. Certainly not bloodshed, but still ... something. Try the bedrooms?"

Barbara led them to the room she shared with Jamie. On the threshold she stopped short. She had left the beds unmade, but not in this wild disorder; blankets flung off and twisted around, stains, lipstick marks on the pillows. ... She went over to the bed, feeling dazed and numb.

"I feel like one of the three bears," she said. *"Someone's been sleeping in my bed. ..."*

Claire's face was wrinkled up in fastidious disgust. She said in a low voice to MacLaren, "Hardly the act of a loving husband. ..."

MacLaren said, tight-lipped, "Certainly not casual adultery, Claire. More of a deliberate, gratuitous insult—another attempt to get under Barbara's skin, that's all." He raised his voice slightly. "Don't jump to conclusions, Barbara. Your husband impressed me as a man of integrity."

She said dully, "Jamie and I always had an agreement that if either of us ever wanted anyone else ... but to do it like this, in my own bed ..."

Claire shook her head. "No man alive would do it like this of his own free will, unless he was trying very hard to alienate his wife, and we have no evidence that your husband was. Don't make any hasty judgments, Barbara; this might very well be a charade for its effect on you."

"But where *is* Jamie?" Her voice cracked. She bent over and picked up something on the pillow, let it drop again from limp fingers.

A calculated insult. As if Dana were saying to me, I always wanted Jamie and now I've got him. And in case you've forgotten, I can get pregnant by him—if it happens to suit me, which it doesn't—and you can't!

MacLaren said quietly, recalling them both, "Let's try the other rooms."

Barbara had not been a dozen times into Jamie's mother's room. She led the way inside, but Claire stopped cold on the threshold, her hands going to her throat. She went pale. Barbara started to speak, but MacLaren quieted her with a gesture. He said, "What is it, Claire?"

"Horrible," Claire whispered. "This is the center of it . . . horrible."

"Quiet, Barbara," MacLaren said in an undertone, "don't disturb her. Claire is a sensitive. It's one reason we work together." He raised his voice slightly, although it was still low and even. "Can you tell me any more?"

Claire pointed. "In there . . . something dreadful," she muttered. MacLaren said, "I apologize in advance for trespassing if either of us is wrong, Barbara," and opened the dressing-table drawer at which Claire was pointing. Inside, lying prosaically next to a box that had contained curlers, was an assortment of little bottles. MacLaren glanced at them. "Either your mother-in-law is a hypochondriac, or else—no, these aren't legitimate prescription bottles," he said slowly. "Evidently she has access to some illegal drug source, an irresponsible or unethical doctor or pharmacist. There seems to be a little of everything here, from aconite to ergot." He gave a mirthless laugh. "The modern pill-peddler has taken the place of the old wise-woman pounding out her herbs and simples, although I'm not sure which one was worse. . . ."

"But Jamie's mother is never sick," Barbara said, confused. "I've never known her to spend a day in bed, and she doesn't even take vitamin pills!"

MacLaren said dryly, "I doubt if she takes these herself. A harmless-looking little old lady might keep the drug hoard for the whole gang of them." He turned the bottles over in his hand. His face contracted and he picked up a bottle three-quarters full of tiny orange pills.

"Barbara, did she ever give you any of these . . . for a headache, maybe?"

"I've never seen them before. Besides—for goodness sake, Mr. MacLaren—I know enough not to take other people's prescriptions!"

"I wonder how she got them into you," MacLaren said. "Recognize them, Claire? Remember that poor devil in Berkeley, who was so glad to be even halfway free of his migraines that he didn't even tell his doctor about the side effects?"

"What are they?" Barbara asked.

"Methysergide," said MacLaren. "Also known as Sansert. First marketed as a miracle drug for migraine. A distant relative of LSD—but LSD is positively good for you, compared to this stuff! Nine-tenths of the people who were on it for more than a few days developed high blood pressure, gastric disturbances, menstrual irregularities—and miscarriages—in women, impotence in men, and all kinds of psychotic freak-outs. Especially the psychotic freak-outs. It was never much more than an experimental drug, and it's not prescribed anymore—legally. Most reputable doctors have given it up. A few crooked drug jobbers sell it for the lysergic acid content: some of the college-kid chemists bought it to break it down and make LSD out of it. It's also a nice thing to poison somebody with, if that person has no idea he's getting it and no medical supervision. Clever—diabolically clever, and horrible."

"Are you trying to tell me Jamie's mother uses *drugs*?"

"I don't know if she *uses* them," MacLaren said dryly, "but she's certainly *got* them—enough to poison half the city. I'd telephone the police, if I were sure it wouldn't hold us up just long enough to risk—" He bit his lip, thinking deeply. "No. Can't risk the delay. Wonder what else is here? Benzedrine and methedrine—speed, the modern witches' brew—and sleeping pills. God knows what other devil's stuff." He looked up at Claire. "I've a good notion just to flush the whole lot down the toilet. She certainly can't complain to the police or report them stolen!"

"Sounds like a great idea. I'll help," Claire said, but she frowned. "Something else . . ."

Colin MacLaren said, "Guide me, then," and began slowly circling the room as Barbara watched in amazement. Claire said suddenly, "There. Lower—no, a little higher than that, not on the floor. . . ."

MacLaren opened the closet, rummaged among the shoes there and pulled out, with surprise, a small reel-to-reel tape recorder. "This, Claire? Looks harmless enough."

But Claire's face was contorted, and she refused to touch it. MacLaren touched the "play" button. The room was suddenly filled with hideous sounds: squeaks, rustlings, odd scraping and scratching, ugly small yelpings. MacLaren frowned.

"Have I been wrong all along?" he asked himself. "Is the old woman just a victim, then . . . maybe a hostage for Jamie's good behavior? Barbara, is your mother-in-law particularly afraid of *rats*?"

Barbara said, with an indrawn breath, "No, but funny you should mention it. It's Jamie's one real phobia; in a prison camp in Korea he had some kind of awful experience with them. We went to some harmless movie about crime on the waterfront once, and in the movie the detective and his girl went down into the hold of a ship, and there were rats in it. Jamie got up and almost ran out of the theatre. He was white as a sheet and I thought he was going to faint."

"So it's for softening *him* up," MacLaren said softly. He put the tape machine down and frowned at it. He said, "Claire, does anything strange strike you? It's Barbara who turns out to need our help, and yet this very same week . . ."

She nodded. "There couldn't be *two* melodramas of that kind connected with one household; they've got to be connected somehow. But what's the missing link?"

MacLaren picked up the tape machine between his hands again, deposited it in the middle of Mrs. Melford's narrow bed, and dusted his hands off. He said quietly, "I feel dirty after touching that. God forbid I should judge any man or woman sight unseen, but it looks as if she was simultaneously trying to poison her daughter-in-law—or at least break her health down—and terrify her son. But why? Why? What's the missing link?"

Barbara said harshly, "I can believe Mother Melford would try to—to drug me. But I can't believe she'd hurt Jamie, I simply can't!"

"It seems unlikely, and yet . . . and yet—no, there's a link that still eludes me," MacLaren said. Abruptly, his voice tense, he said, "Let's get out of this room. It makes me feel a little sick. Do you feel it, Claire?"

Claire said low, her eyes half closed, "Yes. Madness, and hate. Fear. Love turned sick, twisted. And something else, something else . . . someone else, another woman here. A sickness in both of them. I—I think I'm going to be sick," she concluded suddenly and bolted out of the room, dashing unceremoniously to the door of the bathroom.

MacLaren guided Barbara gently to the door and thrust her outside. He drew a piece of chalk from his pocket when the door was shut and, murmuring some quiet words to himself, chalked up a carefully drawn sign in the center of the door. It was almost invisible against the white paint. Seeing Barbara watching, he said quietly, "A pentagram. It may keep the evil in that room from affecting us out here, and it may make it harder for her to get in again. If she walks in on us, she may give herself away." He listened to the sounds of retching from the bathroom and shook his head ruefully. "Poor kid, she hasn't learned to guard herself against that sort of thing yet."

"Are you trying, in all seriousness, to tell me that Jamie's mother is—is mixed up with all those horrible things Jock was trying to expose?" Barbara demanded, but she really no longer doubted it. She realized, suddenly, that she had known it, with some deep inner knowledge, ever since she had found the obscene charm in her bed. She said aloud, "I wonder if Jock knew?" and saw MacLaren's face catch a light.

"I don't know, Barbara, but it could very well be, and that could be the missing link."

Claire came out of the bathroom looking white and drained. She said weakly, "Sorry, Colin, it just all hit me at once. I won't do it again."

"You'll learn," MacLaren said. "I hope you're all right, Claire. We've made the diagnosis, but now for the treatment—we haven't a clue where these people are, what they're doing, where James Melford is, or how much time we have. They've already killed one man we know about, so there isn't any time to lose. Once they get a hint we're on their trail, there's no telling what they'll do next."

"I'm all right now." Claire followed them into the living room. She said, "Did you seal the bedroom door?"

"Yes, although with the lesser pentagram. I'm not sure it will hold anyone out or in, but it might keep us from being affected by the atmosphere in there," Colin said. "Get the suitcase open, will you?"

Barbara listened, irritated by the cryptic words. She said sharply, "Why not simply call the police?"

"And tell them what? And ask them to do what, and where?" Colin demanded, eyebrows raised. "That's the trouble: people of this sort have one thing going for them, that normal people simply don't believe any of it, not until they see it—and sometimes not then. Can you honestly see me calling the police and telling them that these people, whoever they are but possibly including your mother-in-law or some friend of hers, have killed one man with witchcraft and are starting in on someone else, so will the police please lock them up before they can get on with it?"

Barbara bit her lip. "Didn't you just tell me they were poisoning me? I could swear out a complaint."

"Proof. There's a thing call proof," he said almost absentmindedly.

Claire broke in. "Barbara's doctor can confirm——"

"Yes. We may come to that eventually, if everything else fails. But it's a matter of time, you two. By the time we could get a warrant, and an arrest, someone could be dead. Remember, they've already killed Jock Cannon. And I'm not happy about Melford—Jamie, that is—disappearing like this. They may suspect that we're onto them."

"How could they know when we didn't know ourselves till then?"

"The same way Claire found the tape recorder," MacLaren said. "No coven worth the name is without a sensitive or two. They've come out in the open, laughing at Barbara on the telephone and disappearing with Jamie. If they were still covering their tracks, they'd have bullied him into leaving a note saying, he was going to Westchester—or San Francisco, or Khatmandu —on business or taking a client to lunch."

"Then what can we do?"

"God knows—and I'm not being flippant; He knows but we haven't yet been taken into His confidence. Claire, it seems to be up to you. I'm sorry, after what that room did to you, but I'm simply not a good enough clairvoyant, and I may have enough on my plate, as the British say, before the night's over."

"I don't mind," Claire said. She snapped open the suitcase. "Good thing I brought the crystal. I *can* use a bowl of water, but I'd hate to have to look in any bowl that woman had been using!"

She took out something wrapped carefully in a square of black velvet and unrolled it, disclosing an inner square of white silk. Inside that was a small globe of glass or crystal.

"Barbara, love, can you get me a paper towel from the kitchen?"

Somewhat startled, Barbara obeyed. "But wouldn't you rather have a dish towel?"

"God forbid," said Claire, taking the roll of paper toweling and unwinding it slightly to tear off a clean square. "Who knows who's been handling them or what they've been used for? The invention of paper towels and Kleenex was a great boon; this stuff was packed at the factory and it's as neutral as a hunk of wood. Nobody's ever touched it before, nobody will ever use it again, and it won't hold magnetism worth a cuss anyhow." Carefully, with the paper, she wiped off the surface of Jamie's desk, moistened a second square with water from the bathroom and cleaned it carefully, then dried the desk again with a third towel and laid the black velvet on it. Shading her eyes, she looked into the depths of the crystal.

Barbara sat motionless, watching, half moved to laughter, and yet, in view of the absolute seriousness on the faces of both the others, taking it seriously against her will. A small shiver crawled up her spine as the minutes lengthened. Claire's face seemed smoothed out into an impersonal mask, so deeply abstracted that it was almost inhuman. Barbara had the artist's eye of her profession, and this total blotting out of expression and individuality was new and, in spite of the tension of the situation, fascinating.

Time crawled by. Once Claire's face brightened momentarily and Barbara, her eyes fixed on the crystal, seemed to see small shadows moving in the depths, but then the color vanished. At last Claire stirred and moved cramped muscles.

"Nothing," she said wearily, "Either they're over water or I can't pick them up on my own. I wish I could be absolutely sure Barbara's husband didn't willingly join up with them."

Colin said slowly, "I think you can take that for granted. All right, we'll have to use something of his to trace him. If he's not with them, we'll start over. Barbara, get me something of your husband's, preferably something he uses or wears almost every day."

Barbara went into their room, looked around quickly; her eyes fell on the monogrammed silver-backed hairbrush she had given him before they were married. It still had a few of his hairs clinging to it. She carried it back, and Claire said, "This is perfect. Silver holds personal magnetism better than almost anything else, and with his hairs in it——"

Barbara blurted out, "Then all that voodoo

stuff about hairs and fingernail clippings isn't just drivel."

"Not entirely," Colin said. "It's true that anything of a person keeps his magnetism, his vibrations if you like, just as a scientist can unwind the whole genetic code of an individual by the DNA in one cell from his body. Claire's like a radio receiver just now; the brush has Jamie's vibrations and that helps her tune her frequency to station Jamie, so to speak."

Claire, lifting her head, said, "I'm wondering why they suddenly decided to blow their cover just now. *Could* they have discovered that we were on their track?"

"Nothing's impossible. More likely Mrs. Melford discovered that Barbara hadn't followed instructions in going to the psychologist she recommended."

Claire said, hard-faced, "I've had my suspicions of that quack for a long time." She took the hairbrush and laid it on that white silk, just touching the crystal ball. She said, "With this I should pick him up even over water. It isn't as if any of the rivers around the city were clear running water; that might cut me off. Maybe pollution has some value after all? But how do we know he's even in the five boroughs?"

"Seems unlikely they'd have taken him out . . . time element."

"One of them might have a place in Westchester or Connecticut . . . privacy."

Colin MacLaren said irritably, "We have to start *somewhere*, don't we? Let's make sure he's *not* being held in the city before we begin to borrow trouble."

Barbara watched as Claire bent her head again

over the crystal. It seemed incredible, but Claire seemed to take it quite for granted. For that matter, so had Jock Cannon. Was it true then, objective hard fact, that with Jamie's silver-backed brush, some of his hair, a crystal ball, and her own trained mind Claire could—how had MacLaren put it—tune in to station Jamie?

As true as my own death, Barbara. It seemed for a moment that Jock Cannon had whispered these words into the room, and Barbara shivered, then told herself frantically not to start imagining things.

Again the silence grew in the room, and time crawled by, with minutes of silence lengthening and Claire's face smoothed to inhuman effort.

Then, abruptly, her face changed. She murmured, half aloud, "I'm getting something . . . dark room . . . traffic sounds outside . . . hangings, double-cube-shaped block . . ."

Barbara started impulsively; MacLaren gestured her to silence. He said in a very quiet voice, "Is it an altar, Claire?"

"I think so." Her eyes were glassy, fixed motionless on the glow of the crystal.

"Is there anyone else there?"

"Not just now, but I can hear them in another room . . . a red light flickering outside coming and going . . . fire? No, not fire, a neon light just outside the window . . . lots of heavy trucks starting and stopping . . ."

MacLaren asked softly, "Is it in the city, Claire?"

"Sounds like it. Yes, near a big intersection . . . sirens . . . He's tied up, I think, or fuzzy enough not to move on his own—not unconscious, but fuzzy . . ." Her voice trailed away.

"Can you get a direction?"

"No, but I hear . . . a big thump and a rattle, something like blasting." She frowned, her brows furrowed. "And sirens again, again . . ."

She slumped back against the cushions, letting the crystal fall free and roll. Colin MacLaren got up out of the chair, went quickly over to her, and lifted her limp wrist. Then he let it go, sighing in relief. Claire moved slightly and said, "All that isn't much help, is it?"

"It could be," Colin said. "We know it's not any quiet residential district. Do you remember how big the room was?"

"Oh, enormous. Fifty or sixty feet, and a huge, echoing, high ceiling. I heard the echoes."

"A loft, then, or warehouse room," MacLaren said, "near a firehouse or police station—the sirens—and trucks stopping and starting, and blasting going on. Let me use your phone, Barbara." He picked up the receiver and dialed. "Hello, Sergeant? Let me speak to Lieutenant Farrens, please." He waited for several minutes. "Hello, Joe? Listen, can you do me a very small favor? No, not a ticket. Do I ever ask you to fix a ticket? Can you tell me where in the city a blasting permit was issued tonight? Mmm, I see." Blindly he thumbed a notebook out of his pocket, gestured for a pencil; Barbara put the one from the telephone pad into his hand and he scribbled. "Right. No, sorry, I can't tell you about it just now, but nothing illegal—nothing I'm doing, anyhow. I'll tell you about it sometime. How's Edna? Oh, fine. Kiss the baby for me, will you? Okay, Joe. Yes, I am in a hurry, thanks a lot."

He replaced the receiver. "There are some good

things about having a couple of friends on the police force who know I'm on the level," he said. "Joe told me there are only two blasting permits in the city tonight, which means we check them both out for a lot of truck traffic and a nearby firehouse. Two sirens inside of three minutes means a lot of emergency traffic and probably means a busy firehouse. Come on, Claire, are you all right to walk again?"

"Sure, I'm fine. Had I better leave the ball out?"

"Yes. Pocket," MacLaren said, and Claire drew on her coat and thrust the crystal, wrapped in its silk, into her pocket. Barbara pulled on her coat again in a daze. MacLaren hoisted the small suitcase. He said as they went out, "I knew they wouldn't be blasting at night in a residential area, so it had to be a business district."

"Farrens," Claire said. "Is that the officer who had the poltergeist in his house smashing dishes until he didn't have a glass left for the kids to brush their teeth in?"

"No," MacLaren said, hurrying down the stairs. "*He* lived out in Levittown, and I had to do a full-scale exorcism on the place. That one was unholy! No, this was a chap—a friend of the Levittown guy—who kept hearing voices in his apartment until he and his wife were almost crackers. I checked it out and I heard them too, but I didn't *feel* anything. That was while you were away last year, Claire. I used Betsy for a check reading, and she didn't feel anything either. So I went all over the place with a fine-tooth comb, and what do you think I found?"

"A ghost?" Barbara hazarded.

MacLaren laughed. "Not a bit of it; the place

was a perfect whispering gallery, and they were hearing the voices of TV soap operas from the landlady's apartment five floors away in the basement. Since they never heard anything from any nearer apartment, it had never occurred to them they could hear anything further away. I had them change the acoustics of the place by some new curtains and a couple of screens, and they were so glad not to be sent either to a priest or a psychiatrist that I made two friends for life."

He opened the door of the panel truck and ushered them in, slammed the door, and started off, taking a fast route to the East Side. It was very dark now, and icy cold. Barbara shivered, gripping the door handle and staring into the dark at all the Christmas-lighted windows. MacLaren's matter-of-fact account of how he had checked out all the material facts before assuming a haunting had removed her last doubts. Here was no self-deluded lunatic ready to assume some ghostly cause for anything, but a hardheaded skeptic—and he was ready to try anything, once convinced of some inhuman malice. She shivered again. Jamie was somewhere in that night, drugged, captive, at the mercy of some unknown people who had killed once and who, MacLaren took it quite for granted, would not hesitate to kill again.

She tried to tell herself that Mrs. Melford would not allow anyone to hurt Jamie. But to her own horror she discovered that she was no longer even very sure of that.

Chapter Thirteen

THE ROOM WAS DARK AND DIRTY, WITH SPIDER-
webs clotting the corners, almost invisible
in the light of a few dim candles. The smell
of incense was suffocating.

Jamie's first awareness when he began to come
to himself was of the smell of incense and the
dirt and smell of dust in the room. He was lying
facedown on a piece of thick carpet that he
could not see. Outside there were traffic noises
and distant sirens, and he sat up slowly, shaking his head from side to side, then wincing at
the pain.

How had he gotten here? The last thing he
remembered, he was in bed with Dana—how
had that happened? He hadn't really wanted
her, he remembered thinking that he hadn't
wanted her. *Oh, come on, you're a grown man,
you can't say the damn woman hypnotized you!*
She'd kept crooning and muttering in some
strange language, and she'd been wild, her body

feeling as hot as fire, and once she had bitten him and drawn blood. And then ... then what? Then nothing except vague sleepwalking memories of icy wind and a fast swaying sensation and the sound of sirens, his feet moving on rickety stairs, someone laughing, a high shrill peacock sound, the shock of his mother's face in the darkness—*had that been part of the nightmare?* —and then a slow, sick spinning, and he had sunk into unmitigated darkness, where there weren't even any dreams. And then waked here. But where was here?

It occurred to him to wonder—if he had been brought here unconscious, drugged, or hypnotized—if he was a prisoner. Was there, for instance, anything to keep him from getting up, walking out, and taking the first taxi back home? He felt in his pocket ... wallet apparently intact, but no house keys. Well, Barbara would be there by now ... Barbara! Was all this laid on to lure him away while they—that mysterious, all-pervasive *they?*—did something to Barbara?

He tried to sit up, but the room went tilting in slow, graceful circles around his head, and he lay back, realizing he could not yet organize his thoughts enough to stand up. Apparently he wasn't tied up, though, and that was something.

Calm down, Jamie. Think.

This had to have something to do with—what else?—the melodrama into which the death of Jock Cannon had plunged him. Was it less than a week ago? He remembered, with disquiet, the attack of the rats in his apartment. Had they been real or hallucinations? Had he been brought here for the purpose of subjecting him to more of the same? Maybe if he knew what to expect, he could hold out. But what had Dana to do with it? How could she *possibly* be part of it all?

Still, it was undeniable that her coming to the apartment had been surprisingly well-timed to take him at a disadvantage.

At about this point Jamie Melford became aware that for some time he had been hearing voices, just out of range, too far away to be anything but an unverbalized rise and fall. Now, at the far end of the enormous room (church? cathedral? warehouse? factory loft?) a crack of brighter light widened, and a tall man's form came through and strode toward him.

"Awake again? That's right," he said evenly. "No, I wouldn't try anything if I were you, you're probably still as weak as a kitten, and there are five of us out there. Not very powerful, maybe, but more than a match for you in your present state."

Without surprise, but with a curious sense that all the loose pieces of the jigsaw were slipping into place, Jamie recognized the big man's voice and walk. "Mansell," he said aloud. "Then it *was* you I saw with Dana, and I didn't believe my eyes. Of course, I didn't believe it of her either."

"Oh yes. At that point we were still hoping you'd see reason about the book and that we could keep undercover," Mansell said. "Too late for that now."

"For your information, you had me completely taken in. I thought you were one of the victims. Not one of the . . ." Jamie searched for a word, gave it up.

Mansell hunkered down beside Jamie. He was wearing a voluminous dark robe, which, bunched

up around his huge shoulders, gave him the
silhouette of some evil bird. He shrugged. "We
had to sound you out. Oddly enough, the one we
serve prefers willing servants, not slaves, and
you are in a position to be as useful to us as
your friend Cannon."

"You'll never get me to believe Jock was one
of you!"

"A misconception. I should have said, as your
friend Cannon could have been to us, if he had
been willing to see reason. Unfortunately he had
been brainwashed by some sickly conception of
his duty toward humanity, or one of the other
idiotic concepts that prevents man from anything
resembling enlightened self-interest," Mansell
said with a frightening detachment. "Possibly it
was only that his wife shared the driveling superstition in which I was brought up."

"Or could it be that he didn't especially believe in intimidation and murder?"

Mansell sounded uninterested. "He would have
been neither intimidated nor murdered if he
had seen reason," he pointed out, "and what
we did to others was none of his concern."

Jamie felt a curious surge of disbelief. This
character was just too unconcerned to be *real!*
"You sound like the heavy in a kid's comic," he
said, wondering. Then the memory of the moment in the coffee shop, where Mansell had
slipped away and returned with his eyes glittering, came back. "Of course," he said in digust.
"Is it speed or horse? No wonder these freaks
have you on a string!"

Mansell made a quick, menacing move. "I'm
not concerned with your narrow-minded prejudices——"

"The proper word is *bourgeois* prejudices,"
Jamie said. "All one word, like damyankees down
South."

Mansell struck him, not very hard, across the
face. "The first thing for you to learn is how to
speak to me," he said, "and you will learn it,
never fear. You can cooperate willingly or unwillingly, but you will cooperate. Before the night
is out, you will be one of us ... willingly, as I
say, or unwillingly. There is no longer any question of failure or refusal. Tomorrow morning
Cannon's manuscript will be destroyed—by you,
I may as well add."

"Over my dead body, damn you."

"Oh, no," Mansell said indifferently, "you don't
even have that option. The only option is, do
you join us and do all these things with your
faculties still intact and your own willpower
and strength, or do you continue to resist us and
have your mind be wholly wiped out, so that
you walk around like a zombie, with any one of
us who has a use for you controlling you for the
moment?"

Jamie struggled against the drugged lassitude
of his limbs. He could hardly move through the
overwhelming sluggishness. "You filthy damned
bastard—"

Jamie.

It was like an audible, literal whisper, and the
hair suddenly rose on Jamie Melford's forearms,
for the voice was the voice of Jock Cannon.

Jamie. Don't antagonize him.

It was another trick, Jamie thought in sudden, mobilized rage. *They've hypnotized me to
hear Jock's voice and make me cooperative. But
Jock is dead!*

Jamie. Listen to me. These people have no power over me. They could kill me, but I kept my mind and soul free of their power. Look at him. He knows I am here but he cannot hear me.

Indeed, Mansell had rocked back on his heels, looking around him with quick, strange glances, uneasy and sweating. Jamie said, "What's the matter, Mansell? Still thinking about your damnation?"

"Shut up if you want any options at all," the ex-priest snarled.

Stall him, Jamie. Stall him. Keep him talking. Once they start I can't help you. You'll have to help yourself.

It was a good idea, Jamie thought. *Maybe I can keep this kook talking until my own strength comes back and the drug wears off. I don't believe for a moment that I'm hearing Jock's voice, but if it's my own subconscious, it's right on the button.*

He said slowly, "What are these options, then? Are you giving me the chance to join in your— what do you call it? Devil worship? Witchcraft? I never was one for buying a pig in a poke, and all you did the other day was try and scare me. Suppose you tell me . . ." He searched for a reasonable question, compromised on, "Tell me, what's in it for me?"

Mansell's face took on a fanatic light. "We can give you everything you have ever wanted."

Yeah, Jamie thought, *and you're one hell of an advertisement for how the devil pays his servants. For you, the world and everything in it boils down to a needleful of dope every few hours. But keep talking, man. Right on, Jock. I'll keep him talking.*

"Tell me more," he said, and saw Mansell's face looming over his in the darkness.

*   *   *

MacLaren's panel truck swung around a corner, then he twisted violently at the wheel to avoid a wrong-way turn into a one-way street. "Blast," he muttered, "I'm lost. I never did know this area any too well. But there are no warehouses or empty buildings around here, as far as I can tell. It's all small shops and bars and shopping centers, and I don't have any feeling—" He broke off, helpless to explain. "We'll have to try the other blasting site, and it's down in Lower Manhattan. You don't feel anything here, do you, Claire?"

She shook her head, gazing at the street crowded with drunks, hordes of roving adolescents, late Christmas shoppers. "Not that I could sense anything here."

"The area you felt before—it was quiet, not like this?"

"Quiet, yes. Lots of traffic noises but no people noises."

"Okay." He swung the truck again, while Barbara clutched the window frame. "Straight down the East River Drive, I guess. Faster. I know it's nobody's fault, but blast it . . ."

"Not your fault, either," Claire said quietly, "and if you smash the truck up we can't help him anyhow."

In the dark car his face was drawn. "I know. Thanks. But I can't get over being sure that it's a matter of time. And all this time lost up here . . ."

The truck screamed onto the East River Drive and headed south, swerving madly in and out of the heavy flow of traffic.

Barbara whispered, half to herself, "What can we do? What can we do?"

Claire said in an undertone, "Colin's doing all he can. Pray, if you want to. There isn't much else anyone can do just now."

Barbara stared out over the lights of the river, her throat aching. *Claire said "pray" as if it was a normal and helpful thing. And I don't know how.*

I wish I did.

"It a question of power," Mansell said. "Not the phony, Mickey-Mouse thing you get in the church I came from, but the real thing, power you can *feel*. The one real drive all humanity shares, the one the other wants and human drives are all about. Power. To speak and see others do your bidding. To pull strings and make the world jump."

Yes, Jamie thought, *and to have to sneak around dirty warehouse lofts in the dark, and use drugs?* He said, "I've never had any great desire to pull strings and make anyone jump."

"Who do you think you're kidding? What else would have sent you into the publishing business?" Mansell sneered. "Power, the need to make or break writers. The need to influence human opinion. Everyone has it; we simply realize it and aren't hypocrites about it. Listen, if you join us, you'll save your mother a lot of grief."

"You haven't hurt her?"

"Hurt her? Why should I? But she's trying to demand that no harm shall come to her precious boy. She's been trying to recruit you for years," Mansell said. "If you'd married the girl

she picked for you, you'd have been one of us
three years ago."

Jamie realized he was no longer very startled
even at that. Somewhere below the conscious
level, knowledge had been growing in him. Who
else could have triggered Barbara's breakdown?

"Perhaps if I could talk to her," he temporized, but he had overdone it.

"No more stalling," Mansell grated. "Time is
running out; we've got to get started. Either we
begin the ceremony to make you one of us, or
we start the proceedings to keep you from fighting us any further. What is it?"

*Stall, Jamie. Time! Help is on the way, but it
takes time!*

"What would I have to do, to become one of
you?" Jamie asked. "Since I don't especially
believe in God, I'd have to lot of trouble believing in the devil. And some elaborate mumbo
jumbo in which I renounced God and swear
allegiance to Satan wouldn't mean any more to
me than reading out loud from the collected
works of"—he groped for an appropriate metaphor
—"the collected works of Jock Cannon—or Aleister
Crowley—or John Lennon of the Beatles!"

"We don't deal in mumbo jumbo," Mansell
said icily. "What we want from you is a solemn
undertaking—with all your mental force and
without any mental reservations—that from this
day forth you will not oppose us in word, thought,
or deed, and that you will work with every ounce
of your strength to carry forth every one of our
collective aims."

It crossed Jamie's mind that an oath given
under duress is not legally binding. What was to
keep him from saying anything they wanted,

and then walking out and going straight to the
police? "I have no objection . . ."

No, Jamie. It was as clear and loud as Jock's
own voice had been in his office, that last day. It
was inconceivable to him that Mansell could
not hear it; Jamie stopped in mid-thought to
listen. *No, Jamie, it doesn't work that way. These
people have trained minds . . . they would read a
mental reservation. You can't fool them that way.*

And then Jamie remembered all the things in
Jock's chapter five. The things he would have to
do, the very idea of pretending to go along with
these people who had—admittedly—killed Jock
Cannon by their perverted mental tricks, suddenly turned his stomach.

"Go to hell," he said abruptly. "You're no
advertisement for your boss, whether he's Satan
or Joe the Janitor. I wouldn't join any church
that would have picked you for a priest; I
wouldn't join a Boy Scout troop with you for a
scoutmaster! And if my mother put you up to
this, she can go to hell right alongside you. Do
your damnedest. But remember, I'm going to be
a hell of a lot tougher nut to crack than Jock
Cannon. He was scared—but I'm going to sit
here and laugh at you all the time you're pulling off your black mass or whatever other sick
hocus-pocus your dirty, sick little mind can think
up. So go do your Satanic rituals or whatever
perverted junk your dope-freak mind gets its
kicks with. And get it over with so I can go and
get a bath and wash the taste of all of you out of
my mind."

Mansell's face contorted, and for a moment
Jamie thought he had gone too far, that the
big ex-priest would kick him to death then and

there. But with tremendous effort, Mansell controlled himself and rose.

"On your own head then," he said, and stalked away.

Good, Jamie! You've rattled him! He can't think straight!

Jamie threw one more shot after the departing robed form. "I'll be around when they haul you off to Bellevue in a straitjacket," he taunted. "Do you really think Satan will help you out of that?"

Mansell's shoulders twitched, but he did not turn or speak. The crack of light at the door widened, then was blotted out by his big form, narrowed, and went out.

The panel truck swung off the East River Drive and rattled and bumped over brick-lined streets, half torn up for demolition and replacement. Old shadowed buildings, darkened and without a gleam of light in their lumpy outlines, loomed against the skyline. Far away there was a muffled *Crump-boom!*

"There's the blasting," Claire muttered. "Now to find the right firehouse."

"Somewhere in the glove compartment there's a street map of the city," Colin mumbled. "Dig it out, there's a good girl. Whoever laid out Lower Manhattan must have been freaking out on whatever it was the Indians used, firewater or whatever. I don't think even the taxi drivers know it all."

Barbara felt a curious tension that was almost words. "I think you go this way," she said suddenly.

He looked at her sharply in the darkness, but

said, "Right," and turned the wheel. Abruptly there was a clang of bells and the screeching wail of a siren. A fire truck roared around the corner, clanged and banged past them, and was gone, its red lights dying away up the dark street.

Jamie flexed his muscles, trying in the dark to rise. He wished he knew what they'd given him; he felt as groggy as he'd felt in the Navy hospital on his way back to the USA, when he kept having nightmares about rats running over his friend's body and they'd kept him on heavy doses of tranquilizers for almost a week.

The door opened; through the crack of light came a procession of dark shapes: Mansell, robed and ominous at their head, bearing a dark torch, behind him a lumbering procession of dark forms that he could see by candlelight were all naked, so lumpy, sagging, unlovely, and ugly that the nakedness had nothing even faintly erotic about it. As one scrawny form passed him, though having been braced for it by Mansell's words, shock and revulsion made his stomach turn.

Stall, Jamie!

He groped wildly for words. "Hello, Mother," he said, "isn't it pretty late for you to be out? I guess I'd better get you some new clothes for Christmas; I didn't know Barbara and I were keeping you *that* short!"

He felt the surge of mingled rage and shock from the menacing, naked forms, but he had also seen the spasm pass over her face and realized unerringly that he had touched her somehow.

"Be silent!" It was a deep-throated command, but Jamie knew he was using the best delaying tactic of all. "Come on, Mom," he added, trying to sound lighthearted and hide the tremble in his voice, "you're pretty well preserved, but still no Playboy bunny. Go get your clothes on and let's get out of this lunatic asylum. You haven't got the figure to run around in these togs at this time of year, and think what it will do to your arthritis if you catch a chill."

He saw her step falter. Then Dana was there beside her, her face twisted unrecognizably, her eyes glittering with rage. She gestured, and two men, great lumpy naked shapes with hulking shoulders and big paunches, rushed forward and kicked Jamie in the ribs. He rolled over, clutching his belly, balling up against them—even bare feet can inflict a lot of damage—but he heard his mother's cry of mingled rage and anguish.

Mansell said inexorably, "Gag him."

Two dark forms bent over him. A rag was forced between his teeth and tightened. Jamie choked, tried not to vomit, and felt the gag forcing his tongue back. All his energies went to the desperate attempt to breathe. He felt his consciousness lapsing again, his eyes darkening.

"There's the firehouse," Claire said. "It must be around here somewhere. Where do we look? All these buildings are so much alike. . . ."

"Look for a dim light in a window," MacLaren said, slowing the truck to a crawl. "If they're like any such group I've ever known, they'll need fire in some form—torches, candles—and firelight and electric light are easy to tell apart at a distance. It's deserted enough here that they could be doing almost anything—ah!" he said abruptly. "Look."

Barbara saw only a parked car where he

pointed. Claire followed his pointing finger and said, "I don't quite——"

"A limousine, parked. Look, kids, this is a business district, a factory district. Nobody here now but night watchmen, and show me the night watchman with a car like *that*? And over there, a Mercedes-Benz. Even the lunchrooms for the factory workers are shut now, and there are no bars, so it couldn't be a couple of well-to-do slummers. We're on the trail, all right. Claire, you drive, I've got to get into the suitcase."

Claire slid over; MacLaren got out, ran around to the back of the truck, and got inside.

Mansell's robed form was silhouetted against the dim light. With the torch he carried he lighted candles, placing them in a dim triangle. One of the men, an ungainly, limping shape, picked up the censer and began to circle counterclockwise round the room, intoning something that sounded like Latin. Jamie lay choking, the sound of his rasping breaths seeming almost louder than the muttered chanting.

Claire seized the wheel, then her face contorted. She drew a long, agonized breath. "Colin," she gasped. *"Colin!"*

"Steady, girl. I'm here." From the back of the truck his face peered over the seat. "Yes, I feel it too, but don't shut down on me."

"It's horrible, horrible, horrible . . ." She was almost babbling. Barbara felt an overpowering sickness and shut her eyes, feeling as if the car were swaying under her. Colin was fumbling in the darkness behind the seats. "I'm getting into my robes, and we need something—I have con-

secrated candles here. Claire! don't you dare
faint on me. I need you to guide me the rest of
the way!" But Claire was slumped over the seat,
gasping. Colin said, "Barbara, can you drive?"

"Yes."

"Haul her out of the seat then, and park us
over by the curb. Not too near that fireplug, no
sense getting any more tickets than we have to."
Barbara obeyed, shifting the inert Claire. *How
could Claire have let them down now? She seemed
so strong. . . .*

"We all have our own strengths and our own
weaknesses," MacLaren said. "It's what Claire
pays for being the sensitive she is." Barbara
parked the truck and shut off the motor, struggling with the unfamiliar clutch and stick shift.
MacLaren laid a hand on Claire's arm. "All right,
girl? Come along, then. Find me the right building . . ."

He eased her gently out of the car. He thrust a
lighted candle into Barbara's hand. His other
hand held something long and bulky under his
robe. "Whatever you do, don't let that light go
out, or we'll all be in the soup with a bunch of
crazies," he said flatly. "And pray, if you know
how. This isn't a game, Barbara. They've killed
one man's body and they're trying to kill Jamie's
mind."

The monotonous chanting and the fogging,
acrid incense were beginning to affect Jamie's
mind. It seemed to him that a dully gray haze
followed the chanting, circling figures, building
up a circle of dull fire, shot through with red-
dish glints of smoky haze. The circle grew, more
palpable in color and form with every circling.

At its center the great black altar glowed with its candles: they gave off thick, foggy smoke and a foul smell. Mansell raised his arms and began to intone, *"Kyrie eleison, Sathanas eleison, Eloi Sabaoth, Eloi Sabaoth, Eloi Sabaoth . . ."*

Jamie felt his head pounding with the dizzying smell of the drugged incense and smoke. The chanting went on and on.

Fight, Jamie! Fight inside! Don't listen to it! Don't let it enspell you! Pray if you can! If you can't, think of something, anything else. . . .

Jamie groped for sanity and then, remembering an old story read in childhood, began mentally to repeat . . . the multiplication table! He could not utter a sound, but, trying to shut his mind against the dizzying smell and sound, he repeated to himself: "Four times five is twenty, four times six is twenty-four, four times seven is twenty-eight, four times eight . . ."

"Here." Claire turned aside suddenly and retched sharply.

"This building? Are you sure?"

"No," Claire muttered miserably. "One of these . . ."

A fire engine clanged past, and Barbara, shivering in the icy wind against an inner cold, felt rather than saw the curious glances given to them. Colin, now wrapped in a long, light, hooded garment, made her think of a "hippie guru" she had seen on TV; Claire was staggering like a drunken woman. Barbara said, "I hope those firemen don't think we're out to commit arson with this candle!"

"Hush!" MacLaren said sharply. "Let her concentrate. Claire! *Claire!* Don't let me down now!"

*   *   *

Dana's body, white and glittering and naked, rose up in the firelight. She held in her hand two crossed daggers, and her eyes were like a cat's, gleaming in the light. The chant grew, incessant, endless, like the drip of water on stone.

"Baal, Sin, Ashtoreth, Ahazrael, Adonai, Adonai, Adonai, Adonai. . . ."

"Twelve times eleven is one hundred and thirty-one, twelve times twelve is one hundred and forty-two—dammit—one hundred and forty-four, and twelve times thirteen is—oh hell—one times one is one, one times two is two . . ."

"Zazay, Salmay, Dalmay, Ledrion, Amisor, Or! Great angels and demons of Darkness, be thou present and impart unto these creatures of Earth such virtues . . ."

"Eight times eight is sixty-four, eight times nine is seventy-two, eight times ten is . . ."

"This is the building." Claire was white as a sheet.

"Are you sure, Claire?"

"I'm sure." She touched the door handle, then jerked her hand away as if it were burned. MacLaren jerked at the handle: it was locked. He thrust the long wrapped bundle into Claire's hands and jerked up his robe to get at his trouser pocket. He brought out a ring of skeleton keys and a long thin lock-pick. He said, "Don't let that touch the ground, or the stairwell when we get in. Thank the Lords of Karma for some of the weird things I learned knocking around."

"Will we all go to jail for housebreaking?" inquired Barbara.

"I may. You won't. I doubt if I will after we

find out what's inside," Colin said and began to thrust skeleton key after skeleton key into the lock.

With hard hands they stripped off his clothes, rolling him from side to side. The multiplication table vanished under the rough handling.

One of the women, not his mother, not Dana, dipped a bundle of some rough twigs into a bowl of fluid and sprinkled him with drops of something that smelled foul and felt unpleasantly sticky.

"*Aspergo, aspergo, aspergo . . .*"

"Damn this lock!" Colin's face was drawn and contorted in the solitary streetlight. He twisted delicately, his fingers moving as if under their own guidance. "Makes it hard for a respectable housebreaker . . . *there!*" The door opened inward on a square of darkness and flights of dusty, dirty stairs smelling of ancient grime and cat urine and leading upward. "Here, Claire, I'll carry that—ugh! Feels foul. It's been used for *something*, right enough. . . ."

Barbara stepped up into darkness, feeling her throat constrict. Ahead of her, Claire and MacLaren were two dark, hurrying shadows. She pulled her coat tight with one hand, sheltered the candle with another, and sped after them.

Jamie moved in the darkness and realized that his strength was returning. The unutterable lassitude was gone. He could hardly breathe for the gag, but he could move, and if the chant would only stop, so that he could *think* . . .

They were still circling him inside the magical haze of fire, sprinkling him, muttering. He gathered his forces for a sudden effort. If he could grab Mansell, put out that damned torch of his, and disrupt the proceedings, this crew of crazies, drugged and lunatic as they were, might not be able to cope with his returning strength. He wouldn't try to fight, just to run, get out onto a fire escape if he could manage it, smash a window, and yell bloody murder. From the sound of sirens he imagined there must be either a police station or firehouse nearby ... anything to interrupt the proceedings.

"Zazay, Salmay, Dalmay ... be thou present ... creatures of air, creatures of earth, creatures of fire ..."

Jamie braced himself for a great leap.

Wait, Jamie. Not now. Not yet. Let them get deeper into it. ...

He rolled back, relaxing, biding his time, gathering his strength.

MacLaren halted on the fourth landing. He took from Claire the wrapped bundle and stripped off the wrappings, then gestured to Barbara to give Claire the candle. He said quite simply, "You've got to realize that they may try to kill us. Well ..." He crossed himself and said quietly, "Into thy hands, O Lord, I commend my spirit."

He flung himself, with his full weight, against the door. It burst open. Barbara saw a dark, smoky glow, heard the sound of chanting, and followed him inside, her heart pounding. ...

Jamie rolled over, saw the door burst open and a tall figure, glowing with a blue haze, break into the room and make straight for the dark-glowing magic circle. He raised in his hand a sword, which seemed to glow blue from hilt to tip, and made a cutting motion.

"In the name of God! In the name of the Lords of Karma and the forces of Nature! In the name of the Fatherhood of God, the motherhood of Nature and the brotherhood of Man, I scatter your forces!"

The palpable smoky circle broke, scattered like fragments of fog. The naked dark forms screamed, gasped, and turned on the invader, who stood tall, his arms flung out crosswise, seeming to radiate power and strength. He walked through the broken magic circle straight to the altar; he thrust his body against it and overturned it; he trod out the candles under his foot.

"I spit on the uncleanness of the pit," he said in his clear and resonant voice. "I spit on those who make unclean those things that God has ordained to the use of man."

He kicked over the dish of incense, trod it out, scattered it with sand.

Barbara ran through the screaming, gasping assemblage—only drugged, naked, moaning men and women now—bent over Jamie, and ripped the gag out of his mouth. He rose to his knees and clutched her.

"Colin! Look out!" Claire shouted. "He's got a knife!"

Mansell crouched, coming at MacLaren with hands out, knife gleaming, ready to kill. MacLaren kicked out, an adept judo kick. The knife went flying, but MacLaren's foot connected with the priest's chin. There was a sickening *crunch*; the big man crumpled.

MacLaren said quietly, "Get some light, somebody, if there's anyone here sane enough to do it."

No one moved. The naked men and women stared incuriously, moaning, gasping. Jamie's mother squatted toadlike, her fingers raking in the embers of the incense, muttering. Claire went into the anteroom, fumbled for light switches. The lights came on, revealing the assembled Satanists in all their ugliness. Not one moved.

"Are you still all right, Melford?" MacLaren asked. "Barbara, you're able-bodied and clothed. Run round to the firehouse and call 911, or find a police call-box. I'm very much afraid we have a dead man here." He knelt beside the hulking body of Father Mansell. "Poor devil," he said regretfully, "too bad he never managed to make atonement." He quietly closed the staring eyes, crossed himself, and whispered under his breath. Jamie caught fragments of the words: ". . . my God, I am heartily sorry for having offended thee . . . to do penance . . . and to amend my life . . ."

Jamie said dully, "I didn't know you were a Catholic."

MacLaren's eyes glinted angry blue. "I'm not. But *he* was, and I don't presume to imagine limits on God's mercy; do *you*?"

He heard Barbara's feet on the stairs. She ran back, gasping, "The police will be here in a minute. Oh, Claire! Help me!" She ran to Dana, who was crouching naked behind the overset altar, pulled off her coat, and put it around the girl's bare shoulders. Dana turned on her with an incoherent mumbling sound. Her eyes were blank. She drooled spit down her chin.

Jamie pulled himself upright and slowly, feeling sick, went to his mother. She still squatted, raking the ashes of the fire and muttering to herself. Her eyes were glassy. He said gently, "Mother—Mother, come on, come with me, it's Jamie. Let me get you some clothes, Mother, it isn't decent to sit here like this. . . ."

"Jamie?" she muttered, "not to hurt Jamie."

"I'm not hurt, Mother. Look, I'm all right. Come, let me——"

"Not Jamie," she said, her eyes glazing over, and Jamie looked at MacLaren in amazement. "What's *wrong* with them?"

MacLaren said, "God knows. Drugs, of course, but remember how much of their minds and their—well, souls—they'd put into this—this filthy business." He looked around at the circle of naked men and women, all of whom were staring incurious and glassy-eyed. There were, Jamie noticed, nine of them, four women besides his mother and Dana, three men.

"When it was knocked over, they went into shock. I expect Bellevue is the only answer, just now at all events. You'll have to testify that Mansell was coming at me with a knife," MacLaren said. And then a siren screeched to a halt, and there were the heavy sounds of police thundering on the stairs.

The sun was rising when MacLaren stopped the panel truck in front of Melford's apartment. Claire was asleep on the seat, white and exhausted, but peaceful; MacLaren looked pale and tired, too, but he clasped Jamie's hand firmly.

"I'll drop in at the office in a day or two to look over the Cannon manuscript," he said. "It's possible to warn people against the dangers of this sort of thing without giving loaded guns—mental guns—to deranged people."

Jamie nodded. "You've made a believer out of me," he said firmly.

"I hope to make more than that out of you," MacLaren said, extending his other hand to Barbara. "Your wife is a sensitive, and you—well, now you've had a baptism of fire. We can use people like you. Oh yes," he said, at the look of surprise in their faces, "the battle is over, but the war goes on; it's been going on since the temples of Atlantis got out of hand and the black priests stole the secrets of power. It will go on after you and I and all of us are dust . . . but you'll help. Won't you?"

They clasped his hands and it was a solemn promise. "If you'll show us how. We'll both spend our lives—the lives we owe you—in it."

"It's a good lifework," he said soberly. "It's the oldest brotherhood in the world, good against evil. It's what the churches were meant to do, before they got off the track on power games and mistaking local customs for ironclad moralities. Well . . . enough time to teach you all that when the time comes. I hope your mother will make it, Jamie, but I really haven't much hope. And"—he smiled, suddenly, a benediction—"Merry Christmas!"

"Why," said Barbara, drawing a deep breath of amazement, "He's right! Merry Christmas!"

The car drove away, and Jamie and Barbara, hands clasped, went up the steps into their apartment.

Colin MacLaren drove slowly on, smiling absently at the sleeping Claire.

Colin.

Jock. I suspected you were there. They had no power over you, but I would have failed without you to strengthen Jamie.

Now I can rest. My work is done. Lord, lettest thou now thy servant depart in peace.

Colin smiled, but his blue eyes were full of tears.

Now you know. Go in peace, Jock . . . until next life. Rest in peace . . . brother.

He put the car in gear and drove slowly away.